MAD

ABOUT THE

BOY

KATHLEEN DRUMMOND

Matador
9 Priory Business Park
Kibworth Beauchamp
Leicestershire LE8 0RX, UK
Tel: (+44) 116 279 2299
Fax: (+44) 116 279 2277
Email: books@troubador.co.uk
Web: www.troubador.co.uk/matador

ISBN 978 1780880 969
British Library Cataloguing in Publication Data.
A catalogue record for this book is available from the British Library.

Typeset in 11pt Palatino by Troubador Publishing Ltd, Leicester, UK
Printed and bound in the UK by TJ International, Padstow, Cornwall

Matador is an imprint of Troubador Publishing Ltd

For my dear mum

Many thanks to Wendy, Vicky, Jane, Denise, Maya, Dave, Jake and Abby for all their help and encouragement. x

THE NEXT BIG THING

OVERNIGHT SENSATION TEN YEARS IN THE MAKING

Adam looked at the headlines for what must have been the hundredth time and finally pushed them away. His head was spinning. He felt weak and he had hadn't eaten all day. He closed his front door for the last time and with a huge sigh he turned his phone off. Alone, at last. He let peace descend for a few moments before walking into his small kitchen and pouring a large glass of water from the jug in the fridge. As the icy liquid made its way through him he closed his eyes and for the first time that day allowed himself to relax. He felt as though he had been in the gaze of photographers and reporters – *Paps* – for months instead of just one day. It seemed that every time he moved a muscle another flash would explode intrusively in his face. Everything he said appeared now to be of great interest to somebody- everybody – and was noted down. He sat down heavily on the sofa and lay back. This was what he wanted wasn't it? This moment was what he had spent the last ten years working his backside off for wasn't it? Wasn't this what filled his dreams since he was a very small boy? Every ounce of him screamed back 'Yes, Yes, Yes!' He knew that it was true but then why did he feel so scared?

Adam's debut single *It Must Have Been a Dream* went straight into the charts at number one. His first album, due to be released in two weeks time looked set to follow. The media hype surrounding this new boy wonder was set to ensure that it did just that. He couldn't put a foot wrong, or so it seemed. Adam, according to the UK Press, was just what the music industry needed. After years of manufactured pop/ boy bands and fairly talentless talent shows, he was like a breath of fresh air.

Singer, songwriter, composer *and* musician, Adam had it all and in addition he had looks to send the nations girls (and some boys) into convulsions. Adam could not fail. According to the press he had *come from nowhere* but of course, no one *ever* comes from nowhere. Adam had spent years working towards this point in his career; years of working late into the night, of knocking on doors, of rejection, of almost giving up because he had spent his last penny, years of doubting if he really had any talent or ability at all.

He opened his eyes and placed his glass on the coffee table to prevent the remaining contents from spilling all over him and just before he began to drift towards the deep sleep of the exhausted, Adam took in his surroundings as he had so many times before. He loved his flat. It was small but it was his and it was home. It now felt like his sanctuary. He glanced back over towards the front door to double check that he had put the security chain on as he had let his manager out a few minutes ago. He didn't want anyone else invading his privacy today. He needed to be alone.

Adam slowly got up and walked across the room to turn out the light and headed to the bedroom. He knew that if he didn't go to bed now he would fall asleep on the sofa. Tomorrow morning he would need to be fresh, alert and ready for the circus that now seemed to surround him to start all over again. He threw his clothes off, quickly brushed his teeth and collapsed on his huge white bed. He closed his eyes and waited for sleep to wash over him. But sleep didn't come. His mind was screaming. He suddenly realised *why* he felt scared. The life that he had known, the one where he was an unemployed musician with a dream, the one where he could walk down the road and nobody would look twice at him, where he could do exactly what he wanted and no one took any notice, was gone forever. He rolled over in bed and grabbed a pillow. He held it tight and squeezed it like he would never let go. Sometime later he drifted into sleep, not a deep peaceful sleep but a sleep interrupted by eyes staring at him, by cameras flashing at him and by people reaching out and trying to touch him.

*

Janey took a deep breath and sank back in her chair, staring at her computer screen. For the past month she had been visiting the Adam Olsen Fan Site – AOFS or

OAFS as it seemed to have been affectionately renamed by those who frequented it. She had become quite familiar with the user names of a lot of the regulars but she wasn't confident enough to sign up herself, after all, she was in her forties. The last time she belonged to a fan club was The Bay City Rollers when she was a very young child and she wouldn't be very ready to admit that to anyone these days, but Adam had totally blown her away. She hadn't felt this excited about anything for years. His music was incredible and so very different from the usual dross that was churned out nowadays.

She had first heard *It Must Have Been a Dream* on the radio in the office and right from that first hearing she realised that she was listening to something very special and the musical equivalent of love at first sight. She didn't know who the artist was, or even the title of the song, all she knew was that she needed to hear it again and soon. Janey was in luck as it was played again on the car radio as she drove home that evening and this time she managed to catch his name: Adam Olsen, a new, young singer/songwriter who was about to release his first album.

Later as she sat down to her usual post-supper browsing session, instead of checking her emails first as she usually did she found herself googling Adam Olsen. AOFS came up first on the list and she was soon lost in the heady of world of pop star worship. She clicked on page after page devouring as much information as she could about Adam. She was in love with his music and didn't really care what he looked like; he could look like an old boot for all she cared as long as he continued to sing in such an incredible way. However, he didn't look like an old boot. He was gorgeous. Dark blond hair, cut quite short at the back, longer on top, deep, piercing blue eyes, square jaw, slim but with a nicely defined shape and he had very classy dress sense, as the numerous pictures detailed. On stage, off stage, it looked like wherever he was photographed he was always ready for it and gave a killer smile to the cameras, perfect teeth peeped out from behind full, strong looking lips and in some pictures, designer stubble completed the look.

Janey had never visited a fan site before and was amazed at the number of different topic threads there were. As well as the things she was expecting to find, like information about record releases, forthcoming gigs, and factual stuff about Adam himself there were also other more random topics. She found herself browsing threads entitled 'Adam's feet', 'Adams dog – does he have one?' 'I saw Adam in Sainsbury's' 'Why is Adam so gorgeous?' 'What would you say to Adam if you ever met him?'

At first Janey felt like an impostor. Here she was, a woman in her forties, spending hours reading what must surely be young girls posts about a young pop star. It felt wrong. But she loved his music and his lyrics covered subjects with a depth of understanding that belied his years. He wrote with such passion and feeling that it was almost impossible to believe that he was only in his twenties. But he was – and early twenties at that. Surely it was wrong for a woman in her forties to have such strong feelings towards a young pop star?

That night Janey went to bed telling herself that she needed to grow up and act her age. Pop stars and fan clubs were for young girls and she had done all of that in her younger days. She had moved on now; a responsible adult. She turned out the light and tried to put Adam Olsen and the AOFS to the back of her mind, determining to enjoy his music when it came on the radio but that would be the end of it.

At 2:00am Janey woke up with a start. The lyrics of *Dream* were in her head. Adam was singing to her as she awoke and snapped into consciousness. She sat up and took a sip from her glass of water. Normally she slept well so it seemed odd to be awake at this hour. She placed the glass back on the bedside table and lay down to go back to sleep, but that song wouldn't go away. It was in her brain and it seemed that it was staying in there. After about an hour she decided that she would get up and make a cup of tea to see if that would help. As she waited for the kettle to boil she inexplicably found herself turning on the computer. What was she doing? She was rarely up during the night and if she was, the last thing she would normally do would be to switch on the computer. However, that is what her hands seemed to be doing on this occasion and before she knew it she had logged on to AOFS as a visitor again. The internet being a worldwide concern meant that even at 3:00am there were still people posting, no doubt from different time zones or other insomniacs like me, Janey thought wryly. Janey settled down with her cup of tea and taking up where she had left off the previous evening, continued to extend her knowledge on everything Adam Olsen.

Over the next month Janey's visits to AOFS increased and before the first week was out she was logging in as soon as she got up on a morning just to check what was happening. It soon became routine that she would log in every morning and every evening. By the time that Adams Album was released she had started to surreptitiously log in at the office. The problem was that the background on the AOFS site was a distinctive dark blue with tiny silver stars, so it wasn't easy to hide. However, Janey managed to angle her computer screen so that most of the time no one else could see it.

But now, having spent a month watching from a distance, becoming very familiar with a lot of the regular users and reading everything there was to read about Adam, Janey could resist it no longer. However, she wasn't going to sign in with her real name. That would be too much of a risk. Someone in Real Life might find out about her secret passion. People had all sorts of names on there. Some used their real names (fools!) but a lot had obviously made-up names; *Adam's Apple, Adam's Love* for examp… or lyrics taken for one of his songs *New Lover* or *Phantom Angel*. Janey spent quite some time thinking about what her user name would be, eventually deciding on *Adam's Angel* combining both his name and a reference to one of his lyrics. She was still quite nervous as she entered the sign-up page requesting her username. Cautiously she typed in *Adam's Angel. Sorry, that username has already been taken* came the immediate response. Damn. By whom? She had never seen anyone posting under that name. Someone must have signed up with that name then decided not to post. What a waste. Janey tried again, omitting the apostrophe. Adams Angel. Success! Although she was usually careful about being grammatically correct she could live with this slight transgression, particularly as her real persona wasn't being identified.

Site etiquette dictated new members should begin by posting an introductory thread. Janey didn't really feel like a new member as she had spent the last month eavesdropping other peoples' conversations but she knew that in reality she was. So, still feeling that she would be the oldest member on the site and being sure that she would be ridiculed, she cautiously started to compose her first post:

Hi. As you will see, I am Adams Angel. Not really of course, although I wish I was, LOL. (she had been around the site long enough to know that abbreviations such as LOL meaning *laugh out loud* were in common use and she wanted to try and fit in.) *I am probably a little older than most of Adam's fans but I just love him to bits. I live in the South of England and work in an office. I live alone.* (sad smiley*). I have been logging into AOFS for a while now, as a visitor, but have finally decided to sign up as I can't keep quiet any longer.* (shocked smiley). *No one in Real Life knows about my feelings for Adam but I just can't get enough. Ever since the album came out I have been listening to it constantly, morning, noon and night. I'm lucky in that living alone means that there is no one to complain.* (wink smiley). *Not that they should complain anyway of course as Adam has the most beautiful voice ever created.* (love smiley). *I am so looking forward to him announcing some tour dates. I just can't wait to finally be able to see him and hear his beautiful voice live. OMG, I think I would pass out. (fan-girly smiley)*

She hit the *post now* button and watched as her post appeared on the screen complete with dark blue backing and silver stars. Her first post on AOFS! Janey felt relieved and strangely liberated, as if her secret life was not now quite so secret – it was almost like coming out. She chuckled to herself as she sat back and waited to see if there would be any responses. She refreshed the page.

Hi Adams Angel! Welcome to OAFS. If you have been around a while as a visitor I am sure that you will know that is how we refer to ourselves (laughing smiley). *Well done for posting! I lurked for a while too before summoning up the courage to post. I too am a little older than the average Adam fan – or what we perceive to be the average anyway. Maybe we are wrong; maybe there are lots of us out there that have been around long enough to be able to appreciate real talent when we hear it.* (thumbs up smiley).

The post came from someone named Sarah. She's obviously not bothered about not using her real name Janey thought. Strange that, from someone who says she is 'older'. You would have thought that, like Janey, she would want to preserve her privacy. Anyway, no problem. It was nice of her to reply so promptly.

Janey swiftly composed her response.

Hi Sarah. Thanks for the reply (smiley face). *There was*

I, thinking that I was the only old lady, old enough to be Adam's mother who would be on here. I was a little nervous about posting.

By this time Janey's introductory post had attracted several responses. Many posters offered the standard *Hi, welcome to OAFS* or similar; others told Janey a little about themselves and about their love for Adam.

Having got started there was no stopping Janey. By the end of the evening she had posted over 100 times. Her user title which was displayed underneath her name had already changed from *New Adam Fan* to *Adam Maniac*. Janey felt a little uncomfortable with that. She didn't want to be considered a maniac, but she knew it was just an automatically generated feature that didn't really mean anything.

At 1:00am she thought that she ought to log off. She had work in the morning and it would probably be best if she could function like a human being. This may be difficult if she continued to sit here talking to her new-found friends, oh but it was just so nice to be amongst like-minded people; people who understood that everything in life now seemed to revolve around Adam. She said her goodbyes for the evening, promising to be back the next night and with a contented smile switched off her computer.

*

Sarah giggled to herself as she sat in her deep leather armchair. Her husband, Dan, cast a glance in her direction with that *oh not again* look on his face. That was all she seemed to do on an evening now, sit in that chair with her laptop on her knee and giggle. Ever since she discovered the Adam Olsen Fan Site she seemed to have pretty much a one track mind. He couldn't understand it personally. Fair enough, he could appreciate that the lad had talent, he sang well and lyrically his songs *were* incredibly mature but his Sarah was no young girl and their own kids weren't far off the same age as her new found idol. It seemed a little odd, but he didn't mind really. He was very secure in his relationship with his wife and it was nice to see her enjoying herself. There could be no harm in it surely.

Sarah glanced at the photo that she had just selected then looked over the top of the screen towards Dan. Dare she use this picture as her new screen saver? As a partner he had been very supportive of her new found addiction. It was extremely rare for them to agree about music. In the twenty-two years that they had been married she couldn't really remember it happening before. Their tussles and rows about music and musicians had been one of the defining factors of their relationship. She had often said that if they didn't argue about music they wouldn't know what to talk about. But Adam was different. He had seemed to come out of the blue with a sound so refreshing and new that he had quite simply turned the music world upside-down. Of course her husband wasn't going to enthuse about him in quite the same way as she did; she would be quite worried if he got *that* excited about another guy. But he did appreciate that Adam had talent and he quite enjoyed his music. However over the last month Sarah had allowed herself to be drawn deeper and deeper into the world of Adam Olsen. She had had a picture of him as the background on her computer for a while now but this one took hero-worship to a new level. It was taken against a black background and Adam's blond good looks were shown to their best advantage. The picture was taken on stage and Adam was hot and sweaty, his hair was glistening, highlights gleaming and beads of sweat were running down his face. In normal circumstances that would be most unattractive, but these weren't normal circumstances. This was a superhuman that we were talking about here. He was deep in concentration as he sang, his beautiful eyes were closed and his mouth opened provocatively. Adam looked incredible. Deciding to throw caution to the wind Sarah clicked *save as background*.

Sarah loved the internet. She couldn't imagine life without it now. She had always been a music fan but these days things were very different. There was so much material available at the click of a mouse 24/7. She didn't really like to think about the number of hours that she had spent on *YouTube* looking for clips of Adam. There weren't many available yet as he was so new on the scene, but anything there was, you can guarantee that she had found it. Her list of favourites were growing on a daily basis. She was never happier than when Dan was engrossed in a football game on TV because this gave her the opportunity to plug the headphones into her laptop and lose herself in YouTube clips – and then there was AOFS. It was so refreshing to be able to chat with people who didn't seem to think that she had lost her marbles; people who understood exactly *why* she wanted to spend so much time, looking at, talking about and listening to Adam. People who didn't question *why* she lusted after a young boy – but she *didn't* lust after him. The people who were part of her Real Life just didn't understand but the people on AOFS did. No wonder she suddenly felt closer to these strangers. They may live miles away, they may have never met, they may have absolutely nothing else in common – but they understood. That was all that mattered.

*

Clare let herself into the flat. Quietly she placed her suitcase by the door and looked around. She had only been away a few days but she missed home badly. She knew that her boyfriend was in the bedroom fast asleep and she longed to go in and cuddle in beside him. He had texted earlier to say that he was really sorry but he was exhausted after an incredibly busy day and that he was going to have to go to bed but she was to wake him when she arrived home. He was dying to see her. Clare smiled, both at the memory of the text and in anticipation of climbing in beside him and covering him with butterfly kisses until he roused.

The flat looked great. He loved it as much as she did and he liked to keep it tidy no matter how busy he was. To be honest it was his flat anyway. He had been left some money by an elderly relative and had sunk it all into buying this tiny flat. It was a wise move in one way, property is almost always a good investment. But you have to have money to run a home and this was where his plan fell apart a little bit. When Clare had met him he was unemployed, almost penniless and very nearly on the point of losing the flat. But she earned decent money and on a regular basis, so when they got together they were able to get his financial situation back on track and they were secure now in their home.

Clare went to the kitchen, flicked the light switch and put the kettle on. She knew that she shouldn't have caffeine really at this time of night, but surely tea wasn't as bad as coffee? She wouldn't be able to settle without a cup anyway so she would take the risk. Her business trip had been very successful but so much was going on at home she had just been desperate to get back. And now she was here. She sat on the sofa with her tea, curled her feet underneath her and sank back. So much more comfortable than an airline seat.

Clare's mind was already picturing herself climbing into the oversized bed in the next room. She smiled again as she thought about his warm body slowly becoming aware of her presence, him turning sleepily to face her and taking her longingly into his arms. She could almost feel his hungry kisses covering her face. She placed her cup down on the coffee table, for once foregoing taking it to the kitchen, tonight that wasn't a priority. She was already throwing her clothes off as she walked the short distance across the room and into the bedroom. She didn't bother with a light, abandoning the last of her clothing as she reached the edge of the bed. She gently climbed in and wrapped herself around him. His skin was so warm and soft against hers. She snuggled closer in to him and started to gently kiss his body. Slowly he started to stir and she watched with delight as his eyes opened and he became fully conscious and aware of what was happening. 'Clare-Darling Clare.' He gathered her small body into him and held her like he would never let go. He stroked her softly as he whispered into her hair. 'It's *so* good to have you back home darling Clare. I've missed you *so* much'. Clare felt herself melt in his love. She loved him so much that sometimes it seemed to almost hurt. She drew back a little so that she could see him clearly. She looked deeply into his beautiful eyes. 'I've missed you like crazy too Adam.'

*

'Will you *please* hurry up?' Vara stopped walking again as she waited for her daughter and her friend to catch up once more. Walking home from school, with a friend in tow was not the fastest of activities for Daisy. They were giggling and laughing and doing anything other than concentrating on putting one foot in front of the other. Daisy was very excited about having her friend to stay tonight. Lately her mum hasn't been too much fun. She never seems to have time to spend with her anymore. She just spends all her time on her computer. Sometimes Daisy even has to put herself to bed. Her mum says she will 'just be a minute' and that she will be in to read a story if Daisy gets herself into bed. So Daisy cleans her teeth, chooses a book, gets into bed and waits but quite often mum just doesn't arrive before she falls asleep.

Finally they reach home and Vara dumps her bags as she walks through the flat turning on her computer as she passes. She quickly pours glasses of fruit squash concentrate for the girls although Vara doubts that it has ever seen much fruit. She would love to be able to provide a better diet for Daisy but she just doesn't have the money. She passes the drinks to the girls as her computer springs into life. She has AOFS as her home page so it doesn't take long before she is logged in and settling down.

The front page of AOFS had changed. Instead of the familiar picture of Adam smiling out at her – an image that she always smiled back at as if he could see, she just couldn't help it, there was a bold, striking headline in huge print.

UK TOUR DATES ANNOUNCED

Vara's heart skipped several beats. This is what she had spent the last two months waiting for. FINALLY. Her fingers could barely function properly as she tried to navigate to the correct page. HUH. A month to go before the first date. Another four weeks to have to wait before she got to actually see Adam in person. Still, at least she now had a date to look forward to. Look forward to! What a gross understatement that was. She would be barely able to concentrate on anything else, she couldn't really anyway, even before the dates were announced. So, let's look now, how many of the gigs would she be able to go to? Daisy's birthday was coming up so she would have to try and save some money for that, but surely she would be able to go to at least three? She scanned the list and chose the three gigs which were nearest to her home. Three. Three out of fourteen. She would have liked to have gone to more of course but that just wasn't possible. But surely she could get away with three? Tickets were to go on sale in two days time at 9:00am. Damn. She would have to leave Daisy in the school playground early and run all the way back home in order to be at her keyboard at the vital time. She couldn't possibly risk being late, what if they all sold out within the first five minutes? She began to google the venues and look at public transport. So many plans to make. She ventured into the chat threads and found many other OAFS making similar plans. The excitement level was almost palpable. At last they were going to see Adam for real! What would it be like? Would he be just as good live? Would they manage to get on the front row? Would there be any chance of actually meeting him? If so, what would they say to him?

Soon there were gig threads for all the separate dates. A RSVP facility had been set up at the start of each one. Members who would be attending the shows signed up so that their names appeared on the list and it was possible to see who would be there.

Vara clicked into the 'Oafs Oldies' thread. She wasn't old herself. She was a young single mum. But she liked the atmosphere that she found in there. They were mostly older women who felt a bit confused as to why they had become so totally engrossed in the crazy mad world of pop star worship but were delighted to find that they weren't alone. Those that had set up the thread were happy to welcome anyone of any age and Vara enjoyed the company. It was hilarious sometimes, the topics of conversation in there and Vara had great fun joining in with what were often risqué chats. It had become routine that on Friday nights as many of the Oldies as possible would meet and, fuelled by their individual bottles of wine, engage in conversations that very often resulted in them being warned by the sites moderators. They found this hilarious and Vara could picture each and every one of the Oldies sitting at their computers laughing out loud as they composed ever more daring posts. And then at other quieter times, if Vara was feeling down about anything she knew that she could always find a supportive listening ear in the Oldies. They didn't *just* talk about Adam. It became a real social network and Vara loved it. The friends that she had made in there were capable of giving her a real good laugh, but could also offer her help and advice when she needed it. The Oldies thread had become her online home and she couldn't imagine how she had managed without it.

'ARGHHHHHHHHHHHHHHHHHHHHHHHHH' Vara burst into the thread.

'I see you have seen the dates then. LOL' responded Sarah.

'Yeah, at long last. I just can't WAIT. Which are you going to Sarah?'.

Sarah paused a moment before she replied. She fully

intended to go to a lot of the gigs. Although she wanted to be honest with Vara she needed to choose her words carefully. She knew that Vara was on a very limited budget and she didn't want to appear boastful by saying that she was going to multiple gigs. Neither did she want to encourage Vara to go to more than she could reasonably afford. Sarah was in a very different position. Her children were both working now and she had no dependants. When Sarah's children had been younger they had been her first priority – always. She found it quite sad really that Vara was prepared to spend so much time on OAFS particularly during the early evening when surely her daughter must need her? But it wasn't her position to judge anybody else.

'Oh, I'm not sure just yet, I am just delighted that we finally have some dates. I thought that they would have been announced ages ago, when the album was released' Sarah hit *post now* and hoped that her evasiveness wasn't too blatant.

'Evening ladies' Adams Angel joined Vara, Sarah and a few other excited members.

'Oh, hi AA – dates at last! I just can't wait for Wednesday when tickets go on sale. Which ones are you thinking of going to?' Vara asked.

'HMMMMM not sure..I'll have to sweet talk the boss tomorrow to see how much time I can have off.'

The online conversation progressed as tentative outline plans were laid for travelling, meeting up etc. The hours passed and Vara suddenly realised that it had become dark. She looked across the room and saw the two girls sitting on the couch watching a DVD. With a sense of relief Vara felt less guilty than she would have done if Daisy hadn't had her friend with her. At least Daisy hadn't really needed Vara's attention this evening. She just needed to concentrate on how to get the money for the tickets now. That was going to be the difficult part.

*

Sarah tried to catch her breath. She had flown through her morning routine, pushed the family out of the door, packed her lunch for later, walked the dogs and now she was ready. She had pre-warned them at work that she would be late in. 9:00am what sort of an inconvenient time was that for tickets to go on sale? That was her driving to work time. She had carefully weighed up the options. She could either stay at home and go into work late, or go into work early and risk using the works computer. But they weren't supposed to use that for anything involving payment, not to mention the fact that they weren't really supposed to use the internet for personal use anyway. So, on balance she had decided that staying at home was the safer option. After all, if she decided to drive to work, what if she got held up? What if, when she logged on at 9:10am all the tickets were sold? She couldn't imagine a worse scenario. She *must* see Adam live soon. It was going to kill her having to wait another month as it was but at least she was now going to have a definite date to work to. She had come to accept that almost everyone that knew her, outside of OAFS, though she was completely mad. She couldn't see it herself. She was passionate about Adam's music but she really couldn't see a problem with that. Sometimes, just sometimes, her feelings did begin to overwhelm her a little bit. Like when she simply couldn't get Adam out of her mind. Everything she saw and everything she did seemed to have a reference to Adam. Maybe it was something they had discussed on OAFS or something that she had read about him in an interview or someone who bore a slight resemblance to him. But she wouldn't admit that to anyone. That was her secret. No one could read her thoughts. She hoped. She had been told at work that she stopped typing when Adam's music was played on the radio. She hadn't been aware of that until it was pointed out to her but come to think of it, it was probably true. She had to admit that if she was taking a call and she heard one of his tracks start to play she did have great difficulty in concentrating. But in the big scheme of things she wasn't worried. She had been here before. She had an obsessive personality and that was that. If she was into something she was into in. No half measures. As long as it wasn't a dangerous obsession it was nothing to worry about. She knew that in time, her obsession would begin to weaken. She didn't know when that would be but she was confident that it would happen. In a way that was the only thing that worried her. She didn't want it to pass. She was enjoying it too much. She felt sorry for people who were unable to be really passionate about anything.

But Sarah had to be careful. Her husband was tolerant, he had seen it all before too, but she had to admit that this time *was* different. With the internet, everything was a lot more accessible and to be honest she sometimes thought that the OAFS knew more about Adam than he did. Just about every move that he made seemed to be documented. They were desperate for him to sign up to Twitter so that they could be even more up-to-date with what he was doing, but so far he had resisted all requests to do so. She knew that she was in control of her feelings and that she wouldn't let things get out of hand but she was careful about how much she told Dan. She had told him that she was going into work a little later this morning in order to buy concert tickets but she hadn't told him how many she intended to buy. She would tackle that later and pick her moment carefully.

9:00am, at last. Sarah clicked on the link that had been set up from AOFS to the ticket agent. It wouldn't open. Immediate panic set in. Sarah felt herself start to shake. She tried again. Same result. She couldn't believe this. She had mental images of everyone else being able to access the site and buying up all the tickets whilst she was left impatiently banging her keyboard. She tried a third time. Thank God it worked. The link opened and she saw Adam's name appear. She quickly followed the instructions and bought her ticket to the first gig. The feeling of relief that swept over her was equal to what she had felt when she had received her results for her university degree last year. She had put so much work into her studies, she felt immense pressure to succeed, and she had. It was total madness that she should be experiencing similar feelings now over simply managing to purchase a ticket for a gig. However, there was no time to waste. There were more tickets to buy. The silly site didn't allow multiple purchases. Each gig had to be accessed separately.

At 10:00am Sarah let herself out of the front door and headed to her car. She would certainly have to be *very* careful as to how she chose her words when telling Dan about how she had spent the last hour. She pushed that thought aside as she got into the car. She held her bag close to her; somehow it seemed to give her a great sense of security, knowing that she had fourteen confirmation emails in there. As she set off on her short drive to work she felt happier than she remembered feeling for a long, long time.

*

Adam tried to swallow. He tried again. Somehow it just wasn't working. A huge lump seemed to have taken up residence in his throat. He opened his eyes as reality began to sink in. Today was the day of his first gig since he had become the man of the moment. The last live performance that he had given had been a couple of months ago, before *It Must Have Been a Dream* had been released. There had probably been 100 people in the club if he had been lucky and most of them had just been on a night out, they hadn't gone specifically to see him. Tonight's gig was a sellout. 3,500 tickets sold. 3,500 people eagerly awaiting the first big show from this new Boy Wonder. OK, it wasn't the 02 but it was a hell of a lot bigger than anywhere Adam had played before.

Adam knew, from Clare relating news from AOFS that some of the fans were planning on queuing outside the venue from the early hours in order to get a good position. Adam propped himself up on his pillow just as his phone started to ring.

'Good Morning Adam,' Jason's distinctive Yorkshire accent boomed down the line. Jason had managed music acts for years, from strong, over-confident egomaniacs to talented, nervous newcomers and everything in between. 'How are you feeling this morning?' Jason knew that Adam was nervous about his first big gig. That was understandable, he was a perfectionist after all and he wanted to give his very best. But he had come a long way in a very short space of time and expectations were sky high. That meant pressure. Jason had every faith in Adam whom he had been with for the last six-months. He had overseen the release of *Dreams* closely followed by the album and he had watched as the public's imagination was captured by this breath of fresh air. He guided Adam through the avalanche of offers, interviews, TV appearances and magazine shoots. Jason liked Adam and he couldn't honestly say that of all of the artists with whom he had worked over the years. Some of them were all right but others had very little talent and had just struck lucky. Adam was incredibly talented and after years of climbing his way up, right through his childhood and teens, he had finally been 'discovered'. Jason knew that Adam was incredibly excited about what was happening, but at the same time, somewhat bewildered. Unlike a lot of wannabes these days who just wanted to be famous regardless of whether they had talent or not; for Adam fame was a by-product. He was first and foremost a singer/songwriter and musician. Fame, and money, didn't drive him. His music did.

Although he had no doubt dreamt of being hugely successful, Jason doubted that Adam had ever really believed that it was going to happen. He was a very sensitive guy and always considered how his actions would impact on others. He really *was* the breath of fresh air that the media raved about – but the tabloids had no idea just how accurate that description was. In the short time that they had worked together Jason had witnessed many acts of kindness and sensitivity that were rare these days in any circumstances, much less in the music business. In some ways Jason saw Adam as the son he had never had. Or at least, if he had had a son, he would have hoped that he could have been like Adam. But, he mustn't let sentimentality seep into his professional life. He had a job to do.

'Jason', the name was barely audible.

'Adam!, Good God, what's happened?' Jason felt waves of panic rush through his normally calm controlled persona. This couldn't be happening, what on earth was wrong? Adam had seemed his normal, happy healthy self last night as they had parted company with Adam sensibly heading back to his hotel room for an early night.

'I can't... can't really speak' Adam managed to croak.

'I'll be straight over'. Jason was already half way through the door.

Adam put his phone down and closed his eyes. How did this happen? He had taken such care over the last few days not to do anything that might put his voice at risk. He had barely spoken unless it was totally necessary.

He pictured the scene at the Manchester Apollo. He could almost see all the carefully laid plans coming to fruition. The simple set, the backing bands instruments being put into place. He thought about the pit in front of the stage which Jason had warned him would be swarming with paps. He thought about the fans sitting outside on the pavement. He had been totally aghast when Clare had told him about their plans to get there at 6:00am. He found it almost incomprehensible. Adam didn't dare venture onto AOFS himself. Although he knew that his fears were totally irrational, he somehow didn't believe that he could remain anonymous, even if he just viewed as a visitor. Anyway, to be totally honest, he wasn't sure that he could cope with it. Sometimes Clare told him little bits about the topics that were being discussed on there. It had come as a complete surprise to him that people would spend hours speculating about his underwear for instance. Maybe once he had done some gigs and they had something decent to talk about the subject matter may improve. That thought brought him back to reality with a bump. At this rate there wouldn't *be* any gigs.

Adam opened the door to find Jason accompanied by a doctor. Adam had no idea that it was possible to procure a medical practitioner as quickly as that.

The doctor followed Adam back into the bedroom

and examined him thoroughly. Adam complied when asked to 'open wide' even though it hurt like hell. The doctor took a swab from his throat before checking out his ears and chest. He asked some questions which seemed relevant and some which didn't. Finally he finished his inquisition and stood back. He then asked Adam if he wanted Jason to be in the room for the prognosis. Adam readily agreed as he knew that he was useless at remembering such things and Jason would be sure to ask a myriad of questions the minute the guy had left.

'I am almost certain that your symptoms are psychosomatic' he announced. 'I will have the swab that I have taken analysed and get the results to you as soon as possible. However, I believe that the importance to you of your impending performance this evening has increased your stress levels to the point that physical symptoms have manifested. I recommend that you drink plenty of water, take hot lemon and honey and, if possible, eat some vitamin-C rich fruit. Inhaling steam should also help.' Adam leaned back on his pillows as Jason let the doctor out. He felt so stupid. How could his mind play tricks on him like this?

Jason leant back on the door. He was, of course, hugely relieved but he knew that Adam still required careful handling. If his mental state was such that this could happen he knew that today was not going to be easy. He had seen pre-gig panic many times before. He had also known performers have serious throat infections on the day of huge performances and have to resort to Cortisone injections to reduce inflammation of the vocal chords. That was a drastic measure indeed that many people would not even contemplate due to the possible long term risks to the voice. However, after spending the last hour with worse case scenarios swimming around in his head he now felt able to return to being the calm confident and in-control manager that Adam expected him to be. Remaining in the entrance area, leaving Adam in the bedroom to gather his own thoughts for a few moments Jason called the Crew to see how things were going at the venue. He didn't want to give any hint of a problem and he knew that they would be expecting him to check in. He was just finishing the call with 'Yeah, everything's fine, see you in a bit' as he walked back through into the bedroom.

'Everything's fine apart from the fact that Adam's a basket case and can't even speak' he croaked.

Jason grinned at him. 'Everything is fine once Adam has done as the doc ordered' he soothed. 'No need to rush. Everything is going well. As long as we get there for the sound check by about four there won't be a problem.' The venues ran to strict timetables and Jason knew that they only had a certain timeslot to complete the checks before they needed to be off the stage. However, he didn't want Adam to be there too early as he didn't feel that his stress levels would cope. He would keep him here at the hotel, get someone to bring round the supplies that the doc had recommended and try and create a calming atmosphere. At three he would get the driver to come and collect them. Clare should be at the venue by then which would help Adam to relax a little.

For the first time that morning Adam began to feel a little bit calmer. How would he have coped without Jason? He always knew what to do and how to handle situations. Everyone was giving him, Adam, all the credit for suddenly re-lighting the face of popular music and creating fresh excitement in the business. But where would he be without Jason and the others in the team? Lying in bed with a pillow over his face, that's where.

*

Janey cast a quick glance across to the road atlas spread open on the passenger seat. She had always been a confident driver but she didn't know Manchester at all. She also refused resolutely to have a sat-nav. She didn't care how many people called her old fashioned. She had always coped well with a map and would continue to do so. Sat- navs sent people all over the place, however, she had to admit that it *was* quite difficult to map read and drive at the same time. She didn't want to have to keep stopping to look at the map either. She needed to pick Vara up and get to the venue as soon as possible. She had visions of queues already snaking down the pavement. OK, so it was only 6:00am and doors weren't due to open until 7:00pm that evening. But that was irrelevant. It was Adam's first 'proper' UK gig and the excitement level on OAFS was at fever pitch. She knew some of the fans were flying over from other parts of Europe and that they had arrived the day before, therefore she wouldn't be surprised if they were there already. She had arranged to pick Vara up at

6:30am and then it was just a short drive to the venue. They hoped to be there by 7:00am. Janey swallowed hard again. She was trying to quell the butterflies in her stomach. She was incredibly excited and yet she couldn't really believe that she was doing what she was doing. She had driven half the night to pick up someone that she had never met before to go and stand on a pavement all day queuing to see a pop singer who was half her age. She had tickets to go to several more of Adam's gigs over the next three weeks. Luckily she had quite a lot of leave left this year so she had managed to squeeze in as many gigs as possible. Her schedule was quite tight though. Sometimes she was going to be arriving home in the early hours and having to go to work and appear fresh the following morning. Oh well. It would be fun.

Janey swung her car around a corner and edged her way slowly along the terraced street. Cars were parked tightly on either side and it was only just possible to squeeze down the middle. I hope they don't ever need a fire engine, she thought. She finally pinpointed number 27 and stopped outside. It was impossible to park as the road was completely choked both sides with parked cars. She didn't really want to beep her horn given that it was still quite early. Just as she was deliberating as to the best course of action the blue door of number 27 opened and out bounced Vara. At least Janey assumed it was Vara given that this was the address she had been given. Vara locked the door and bounded up to Janey's car. Opening the door she popped her head in and greeted Janey.

'Hi AA It's fantastic to finally meet you!' She leant across and planted a huge kiss on Janey's cheek. Janey grinned. Vara was as exuberant in real life as she was on the forum.

'Hi Vara, it's lovely to meet you too. Now hop in so that I can move off before I cause a major incident in Dickson Street.' Vara climbed into the car and Janey pulled away. Although the two women had never met in person before they really felt as though they had known each other for years. They had spent hours chatting on the forum, the sessions getting longer by the day as the gigs drew nearer. Janey cast a glance over at Vara as she took a left turn. Vara was very pretty. Although it appeared that she had quite a tough life there was no outward sign of it today. Her short dark hair was shining and her brown eyes sparkling. Her trendy young clothes made Janey feel very dowdy in her plain t-shirt and jeans. But still, they were getting on just fine and the age difference didn't seem to cause any difficulties.

As they pulled up at the traffic lights they could see the Manchester Apollo ahead of them, a former cinema, and now a concert venue where all sorts of people had played. It wasn't a huge venue but it was certainly a lot bigger than the venues that Adam Olsen had previously played. As Janey looked across at the building and got her first glimpse of the fans waiting outside she tried to imagine how Adam would be feeling. Would he be nervous? *She* certainly would be if she had to perform onstage in front of a sellout audience at a place like this. But Adam was a number one selling artist now. Surely he wouldn't feel nervous? As the lights changed and they drove past the building Vara and Janey looked anxiously at the small group waiting outside. How many people were there? At a brief glance it looked like about twenty. Hmmm. Not too bad I suppose, thought Janey. However, she didn't want to waste any time in getting parked and joining the queue just in case there were more people about to descend from somewhere and get in front of them. Vara was of the same mind and as soon as Janey had stopped the engine she was out of the car. They had managed to get a parking space just around the corner but they still felt the need to run the short distance back to the Apollo's front entrance.

Sarah was already in the queue when she saw Vara and Janey approach. She was relieved to see them. She was familiar with some of the other fans already here from the forum but she didn't know them like she felt she knew Janey and Vara. 'Hi Ladies, glad you could make it,' she said, jokingly looking at her watch. 'It's barely 7:00am,' yawned Janey as she hugged Sarah 'and I've been driving half the night.'

'I know. You must be shattered. There's a shop at that petrol station over there, you can get coffee and stuff.' Sarah pointed over at the fuel station across the main junction.

Janey looked in the direction that Sarah was pointing. She would have to give the matter careful thought. She didn't want to risk losing her place in the queue by going off to shops, and more importantly, if she spent all day drinking coffee she would need to use the loo this evening and there was *no* way that she was going to give up her front row position once she was in the venue. She looked around. They were fairly near to the front and under the parapet of the main entrance. There was a doorway with a couple of steps. 'I'll just snuggle down here I think' she said, sitting down and leaning against the wall. 'I may get a drink later,' but she knew she wouldn't. She had waited what seemed like forever to see Adam and wild horses were not going to pull her away from her position in the queue.

*

Slowly Clare walked past the queuing fans. 6:30pm. It was starting to get busy and it was easier for her to observe what was going on without being noticed; not that anyone knew who she was of course and for this she was hugely grateful. She was determined that they, and the media, didn't find out for as long as possible. She couldn't imagine that as Adam's girlfriend she was going to be very popular amongst his increasingly devoted fans – simply because she existed. And she could only begin to imagine the stories that the Gutter Press might dream up about her. There were no ghosts in her attic or seedy stories surrounding her but that didn't usually stop them once they got their teeth into someone. She and Adam were an ordinary couple and she liked it that way. She also valued her privacy and freedom and she couldn't bear the thought of being photographed doing mundane things just because she was Adam Olsen's girlfriend.

She found a spot where she could stand, pretending that she was waiting for someone to arrive, and observed the ever growing crowd. When she had arrived earlier it was much quieter. There had been probably about 100 people lined up outside the doors. The people at the front looked freezing. Some were holding coffee cups, their hands wrapped around them in a desperate attempt to try and absorb the last vestige of warmth from the small vessel. In a way Clare admired their dedication, if she could detach herself from the situation and look at it though neutral eyes that is. They had become huge fans of Adam and they were clearly happy to devote a whole day to standing on a cold pavement in order to get the best position to see him perform. However, she had trouble in detaching her feelings in this way. She had spent enough time on AOFS to know that these people were seriously obsessed. In a relatively short space of time they had become totally fixated with Adam. Not just his music but everything about him. They wanted to know every last detail. So far, mostly because he hadn't performed live or been seen out in public much in the last few months, his personal life had remained private. Thank goodness. But she knew it wouldn't last long now that the tour had started. The OAFS speculated endlessly as to whether Adam was in a relationship and she knew that it would be their mission to find out.

Clare didn't know or understand much about this level of dedication to performers. She had been a fan of a few people, and she still was, but to her that didn't mean effectively running your life around your dedication. On

OAFS she had watched some of these people's obsessions deepen. They were logged on there what seemed like 24/7. They talked about Adam constantly. Where was he? What would he be doing? Who might he be with etc. They made plans about going to the gigs, *all* of the gigs in some cases. This was all new to Clare. If she went to see an artist it was at her local venue. That is what touring is supposed to be about isn't it? The artist travels so that the fans don't have to. Clare would spend the day at work, arrange to meet friends for a drink at about seven then go along to the venue usually getting in about eight thirty after the support band had finished. The concept of travelling all over the country to see the same show night after night was completely alien to her, so now she took what she realised would probably be her one and only chance, cloaked in anonymity as she was, to have a good look at these beings.

The people that she had seen earlier, the ones right at the front were the ones she wanted to concentrate on most. These must be the *real* nuts. She tried to identify them from their forum personas. It would have been useful if they had been wearing name badges she thought. But of course they weren't. To be honest, they looked quite normal really. They were beginning to get a little more animated now. The activity level, and the crowd, grew as seven O'clock drew nearer. That was doors open time. They were now encased behind barriers, erected by the security staff but earlier they had just been standing, or sitting in some cases, chatting quietly. They were a very mixed bag in terms of age. Anything from about fourteen to late forties. They were mostly women with a smattering of youngish guys thrown in. They all seemed very friendly towards each other. Clare wondered if that would continue when the doors opened and they were fighting for the best positions.

She enjoyed standing watching them, knowing that they had absolutely no idea who she was. She toyed with the idea of actually walking over to the barrier and starting a conversation with them. She would have enjoyed that. It would have been a good opportunity to get a sense of what they were *really* like as opposed to how they came across on the forum. She may have even discovered some of their identities. But she knew that it wasn't a realistic option. At some point in the near future they were going to discover who she was and they would then automatically distrust her from the beginning. Although she knew it was going to be an uphill struggle she would like to at least *try* to be polite and courteous to these people who ultimately dreamed of getting her boyfriend into bed.

Like any group of people they were a mix. There were some loud extroverts and some quieter folk who seemed happy to stand back and let the louder characters prevail. They were all getting quite high now. The security guys were pacing up and down the line telling everyone to have their tickets ready and the crowd were anxiously checking their watches every few seconds. Clare focused on one of the older women. She was clutching her ticket tightly in her hand and she must have looked at it about a hundred times in the last few minutes. Clare wondered if she was worried that it was going to disappear if she didn't keep checking it.

She looked a pleasant enough woman, about the same age as Clare's mum really. Clare found that a strange concept and tried to imagine her mum queuing all day to see a pop star. No, that wouldn't happen.

7:00pm finally arrived and the doors didn't open. The front of the queue was now packed very tightly through force of being pushed from behind. Clare could see that friction was rising as people tussled for position. Some people that certainly hadn't been there four hours ago when Clare had arrived had somehow managed to wangle their way forward and were nearly at the front. Those that had been there for hours were, understandably getting very irate and were begging the security guys to intervene. Fortunately, before things could get any worse the doors opened and the crowd surged forward. The security staff had quite a job to hold them back but they were obviously very experienced and managed to get the fans organised so that their tickets were scanned individually and their bags were checked before they were allowed through into the foyer.

Clare watched for a while until most of who she assumed were the most ardent fans had entered the building. She then walked back around to the stage door, showed her *Access All Areas* pass and calmly went back to Adam's dressing room.

*

Adam sat back in his chair and looked around him. The dressing room wasn't huge. Neither was it particularly glamorous, but it was, at least, a dressing room. The small clubs and bars that he had played up until this point had no such luxuries. He looked at the flowers that some of the fans had sent. That was really sweet of them. He appreciated that. He loved flowers and their scent brought freshness and colour to the otherwise stark room.

Now that he was here at the venue Adam felt fine. His nerves had settled and his throat no longer felt painful. He was still a little disturbed at what had happened that morning but with Jason's calming influence and the doctor's sensible advice he had got through it. He had been really pleased with the way the sound check had gone. In fact, it had boosted his confidence. It was strange in a way to be singing to an empty auditorium but it had given him a feel for the size of the place and quite frankly he was now really looking forward to the gig.

There was a quiet knock on the door and a smiling Clare entered the room.

'The throngs are descending' she said as she sat down in a chair opposite him.

'Really? Are they in already?' he asked.

'Well, considering that some of them have been on the pavement since the early hours, I would imagine it can't come a moment too soon for them' she smiled.

Adam grinned in reply. He had managed to get into the building without being detected thanks to Jason's inside knowledge. Adam fully intended to go out after the gig and sign autographs for any fans that waited, but Jason felt that it wasn't in Adam's best interests for them to see him arrive. As much as Adam found it odd that anyone would want to queue all day so that they could be on the front row to see him perform, deep down, he was very flattered. He just hoped that he lived up to their expectations. He knew that most of the papers had reporters and photographers here this evening so the pressure to perform well was certainly on, but he felt fine. He was up for it. He had his routine all worked out leading up to the moment that he would go on stage and so far everything was going to plan. To be honest he felt almost eerily calm. He wouldn't like to try to remember how many times throughout the last ten years he had dreamed of this day; all those nights playing to disinterested pub-goers in sleazy backstreets. Adam knew that he had been lucky to a degree. He had finally managed to get a record deal just at a time when there was a lot of despondency in the music business in general. People were almost crying out for something fresh and interesting and luckily for him he seemed to be just what they were looking for. Of course, he was confident that he *did* have the talent and ability to continue to deliver and that he wasn't just going to be a one hit wonder. Luck had certainly played a part but that was ok. Luck, either good or bad, was a part of life.

The support band were due on at 8:00. They would play for approximately 25-minutes then, when they had taken their equipment off the stage Adam's crew would make the final adjustments to his set. He was due on at 9:00.

*

Clare watched from the wings as the support act started their first number. She felt sorry for them really. She knew that it was a good opportunity in a way for an act to play to a much larger audience than they would normally. But no one was really here to see them and they knew it. To be fair, this audience were ok and were good mannered enough to applaud politely but she knew that they were just desperate for the act to finish as that meant that they were nearer to seeing Adam. Peeping around the side curtain, Clare looked carefully at the front row. Yes, all the faces that had been at the front of the queue were indeed there. That was good. Clare's sense of fairness meant that she would have been very upset if she had seen the faces of the queue jumpers there. Admittedly they were on the second row and Clare wasn't entirely sure that they were justified in that position but at least they weren't at the front.

The support act finished and quickly got their equipment moved off the stage. Adam's crew, who were all experienced roadies, worked quickly and efficiently to move forward the instruments. Clare watched as they taped set lists at various positions around the stage. She was really enjoying this, but she had butterflies in her stomach even if Adam didn't! He was amazingly calm. She had kept out of his way for the last hour allowing him time on his own to go through his preparation. But she knew he wasn't far away now, just far enough back to ensure that he couldn't be seen by anyone in the audience.

The tension was rising in the auditorium. Chants of *Ad-am! Ad-am! Ad-am!* started to fill the building. Clare turned around to look at her boyfriend. She caught her breath. He was standing just behind her and he looked absolutely incredible. If he had been a woman she would have said that he looked radiant. He was positively glowing. He was dressed in a black silk shirt and black trousers. He had a black waistcoat covered with hundreds of tiny stars mirroring the background of his website. His hair has been styled to perfection and completed his pop star look. She looked into his eyes and saw not nerves, not fear or anxiousness but genuine desire; desire to get out there and give the audience what they were so desperate for. She looked at Jason who was standing next to the band ready to give them the go-ahead when he had got the final word through his headphones.

Everything was set. The lights dimmed and Jason gave the nod to the band. They walked out onto the stage, took up their positions and started to play the intro to the opening track of Adam's album. The place exploded. The excitement level was through the ceiling. Adam glanced at Clare and she gave him her broadest grin. She had never felt prouder. She saw him close his eyes and take a deep breath and in the next second he was gone.

Adam was on stage.

*

Sarah leaned on the barrier in front of her. She was absolutely shattered. She barely had a voice left. She had screamed and sung so loudly for the last ninety minutes that she was sure she must have permanently damaged her vocal chords. She had never experienced anything like it. From the moment that Adam leapt onto the stage until the moment he bounced off after the final encore he was like a dynamo. He never stopped for a moment. He was amazing. He performed every track from his album plus some previously unheard pieces and a couple of covers. He came back for two encores as the crowd were going wild. Live and close up he looked even better than he did in pictures. Sarah couldn't believe that she had been so close to him. The gap between the stage and the barrier had been about a meter. He regularly came right to the edge and looked directly into the audience. On a couple of occasions at least she was convinced that he was looking, and smiling, directly at her. At these points she felt as though her heart had probably forgotten to continue beating.

Janey rested her head on Sarah's shoulder. Although they had only met for the first time that day she felt completely at ease in the other woman's company. It was around twenty hours since she had climbed out of her bed and she was totally shattered. The excitement leading up to the gig had kept her going but now all she wanted to do was sleep, and soon. She wasn't even really sure if she wanted to be here, at the stage door, waiting for Adam to come out. They had been told by the security staff that he would leave via this door. She was incredibly nervous. Yes, she adored Adam. She thought about him constantly. For the past few months her life had been run around spending as much time as was humanly possible on his website. She played his music constantly in her car, and at home. She had an embarrassingly high number of photos of him stored on her computer. But to actually *meet* him. This guy had written and sung a number one single and album. He was all over the papers. She had seen him on TV. She had never spoken to anyone famous before. Never even really seen anyone well known up close other than on a stage, and even then, she had never been as close as she had been to Adam that night. He had looked so gorgeous. It had been quite difficult for her to accept that he really was there in front of her. His performance had been brilliant. She could hardly comprehend that he could sound that good live. No producers fiddling with switches to make him sound good, he really did sound just like he did on his album. She had been ecstatic when he smiled straight at her at one particular point. She would need to replay that track over and over to re-live the moment. But still, she couldn't quite imagine what it would be like to actually come face to face with him. Her head still resting on Sarah's shoulder, she shuddered.

Barriers had been erected leading down the side street adjacent to the stage door. The fans had been told that if they stood behind them Adam would make his way down the line signing autographs. Vara clung onto her few inches of barrier. People were pushing from behind but there was no way she was going to let go and let anyone get in front of her. She was desperate to meet Adam. She had fantasized about this moment endlessly, about what she would say and how she would feel. She could barely believe that the moment had almost arrived. But it hadn't arrived. Not yet. He still wasn't here. They must have been standing there for an hour now. How long does it take to have a shower and get changed? What else could he be doing in there? Vara didn't want to dwell on that question. She couldn't bear the thought that there were people inside the building with VIP passes entitling them to actually meet Adam in a calm, controlled unhurried manner. She knew that this indeed would be the case, but it wasn't fair. Why couldn't *she* be there? A lot of those people probably didn't even really like Adam's music. They probably just knew the right people. Life was so unfair sometimes. *She* knew everything there was to know about Adam. She knew all the lyrics of all of his songs. She knew how long he had been with his record label and where he had recorded his album. She could tell you what he liked for breakfast. She could even tell you where he lived. But she wouldn't. She kept that little piece of information to herself. The other OAFS didn't even know that she knew that.

The stage door opened and an audible gasp emitted from the waiting fans. But no, excitement over, it wasn't Adam, just two members of the band. A few of the fans called out their names and they smiled and waved in response, pleased that people recognised them. A few moments later the door opened again. This time two security men emerged followed closely by first Jason and then Adam. Sarah felt her heart jump. She was only about fifth or sixth in the line and Adam seemed to be moving extraordinarily quickly along the barrier flanked by the two security guards. He reached out and took tickets or CD's that were held out to him, some from the people crushed up against the barrier and some from those pushing and reaching over from behind. He signed swiftly and moved on to the next person.

Sarah's turn came. She held out her ticket and managed to mutter 'Hi Adam, please would you sign this?' Adam stopped and looked at her. Perhaps it was the fact that she had actually asked him rather than just pushed something at him that made the difference. He smiled at her and answered 'Of course, what's your name?'

'Sarah' she replied although she wasn't entirely sure how she managed to articulate even her own name by this point. Adam signed her ticket and passed it back to her smiling broadly and moved on.

Someone pushed a camera into the gap between Sarah and Janey and took a very close up picture of Adam. Janey thought this was extremely rude. It is one thing taking pictures of someone when they are on stage but to push a camera into someone's face as close as that was downright obtrusive as far as she was concerned. On reflection Janey realised that it was this action by an unknown person that had ruined her chances of having a special moment with Adam. She must have pushed her ticket under his nose almost robotically because before she knew it her ticket was signed and he had moved on. She watched incredulously as Vara managed to prolong her moment into what seemed like several minutes. Adam was still talking to Vara as he signed other people's items, often without even looking at the recipient. 'Thanks Adam, it was an incredible show, you were awesome' gushed Vara as he finally managed to get away from her and turn his attention to other anxiously waiting fans.

At the end of the line a large people carrier with blacked out windows idled with the engine running. Adam signed the last ticket that was thrust towards him and as Jason swiftly opened the car door he climbed in and with a final wave and smile to the crowd he was gone.

*

18 Months Later

Clare rolled over and shifted her body to snuggle into Adam. Slowly, realisation dawned on her that she appeared to be resting against an empty space. She opened her eyes and her suspicions were confirmed. She sank back into her own side of the bed and sighed. Poor Adam. This was the third night that he had been unable to sleep. However, this should be the end of it now. By the end of today it would all be over and as long as everything had gone well he should be able to rest easy tonight. It was 18-months since their world had been turned upside down by the incredible success of his debut album. Life, for both of them, had changed beyond all recognition. His first tour last year had been a huge success in the UK and had been extended to Europe. He had enjoyed even greater success in mainland Europe than in Britain. As a result of that, tonight he was playing a sellout concert at the Parc des

46

Princes Stadium in Paris. 55,000 people. To be honest, even Clare shuddered at the thought. No wonder he couldn't sleep. The build up to the concert had been exciting and hectic. Clare had left her job in the middle of last year when it became clear that the team surrounding Adam was going to expand. He was perfectly happy for Clare to be involved in his career. It had become increasingly difficult for them to find time to be together. If they were working together at least they were in the same country most of the time which was a distinct improvement on the way things had been.

Clare found him staring out of the window in the sitting room. It wasn't a huge suite in a fancy hotel, just a bedroom and small sitting room in a comfortable, reasonably-sized place. Adam liked to try and avoid the big plush hotels, partly because it was easier to hide in less obvious places and partly because he just preferred the quieter more homely establishments. It was part of Clare's job to book his accommodation which suited her fine as she had a vested interest in finding pleasant places to stay. She liked this hotel. It had been a good find. The sitting room had French doors opening out onto a pretty private courtyard. She poured two glasses of juice from the fridge and encouraged Adam to join her outside in the beautiful early morning sunshine. They sat at the white wrought iron table and looked at one another. There was no need to speak. Their relationship had deepened over the previous 18-months and they could often gauge what the other was thinking without the need for speech. Clare knew that

Adam would be able to cope with today. He just needed the space to do it in his own way. The hard work had almost all been done now. Adam and the band were well rehearsed.

The set was designed and would, by now, be built. Soon Jason would be at the stadium checking that logistically, everything was in place; security arrangements, the crew, the lighting, the sound system and a hundred other things. He would be communicating with the band to make sure everyone was ready. There would, inevitably, be last minute hitches, but Clare wanted as much as possible to protect Adam from them. The sound check was scheduled for 1:00pm. Even allowing for traffic and getting there a little early they didn't need to leave until 11:00. She placed her glass down and plucked a daisy from the little jug of wild flowers on the table. It was so simple, so pure and delicate. She studied it for a while, admiring it's simplicity and beauty then tucked it behind her ear. She shared a love of flowers with Adam and wherever they travelled she always ensured that there were flowers of some description in their rooms.

Adam sat looking at Clare. He was so lucky to have her. The way that his life had changed over the last year was almost incomprehensible. She provided the stability that he needed to try and keep his feet on the ground. It would have been so easy to let his new-found success go completely to his head. Standing on stage looking out at thousands of seemingly adoring faces was one of the best feelings he had ever known. Some of his fans were so committed to him that he honestly felt they would stop at nothing to show there adoration and appreciation. But deep down he couldn't help feeling that it was only skin deep. They professed to love him. How could they love him? They didn't know him. Not one little bit. They loved his music. They adored his stage persona and he was always polite to them if they waited after gigs to see him. But they didn't *know* him. Clare knew him. She knew him almost better then he knew himself. She understood him and knew what he needed and what was right for him.

The success that he was experiencing now was built on his own hard work but sustaining it was just as big a challenge and for that he needed the care and support that Clare irrevocably gave him. She was so tolerant. Some of the fans were quite crazy and certainly weren't shy when it came to expressing their wishes and desires as far as Adam was concerned. He had learned to cope with it but he felt for Clare. He tried to shield her from it as much as possible. Although she worked as his PA he preferred it if she wasn't with him when he met the fans after the gigs so she would wait in the blacked out car. But she knew what went on. Although the fans couldn't see into the car, she could see out. She saw the flirting and sometimes girls managing to get past the security guards and throwing themselves at him. And she still went on OAFS. Sometimes late at night, particularly after the gigs he would glance over at her laptop screen and see the familiar background. He never asked her what she was reading and she rarely said, unless it was to pass on some factual information.

But he had a pretty good idea of the sort of content that was discussed on there and he sometimes wondered how she coped.

Clare looked so fragile in the sunshine. Her frame was small and delicate. To him she was the most beautiful girl in the world and she was indeed his whole world. He couldn't imagine loving anyone more than he loved her. Her lightly-tanned skin seemed to glow against her short white nightie. The daisy that she had just placed behind her ear seemed to define her purity. Leaning forward he gently took her hands in his. He drew her towards him and his eyes closed as he softly kissed her lips. She responded to his kisses eagerly and without opening his eyes he rose, deftly scooping her up in to his arms. Their kisses becoming more and more passionate as he carried her back into the bedroom and lay her on the bed.

Several hours later Adam awoke. He was curled up on the bed with Clare cocooned in his arms. He looked at the bedside clock. 10 o'clock. Perfect. Making love had relaxed him enough to be able to get some sleep and now he was ready to face what was set to be one of the best days of his life. Kissing the top of Clare's head gently he rose and went to shower.

*

Janey was getting good at finding cheap hotels close to venues. Mind you, over the last year and a half she had had some practice. Soon after Adam's UK tour finished a European tour was announced. Then there were one-off concerts here and there. Whenever a gig was announced the same thing happened: there was a mad rush to secure tickets and then all the other arrangements had to be put in place. It was quite hard work being an ageing groupie! Janey only had 25-days leave a year to play with so sometimes she had to be quite inventive with her working hours to try to manage to get to as many shows as possible. She had learnt from experience that it probably wasn't a good idea to arrange to attend meetings on mornings that she had spent half the night driving across the country after a gig, and although budget airlines were a Godsend for the European dates she had come to realise that the bargain prices meant that the flights were generally at times that she would rather not have seen. But it was worth it.

The OAFS community had expanded and developed and she had made some great friends; particularly the Oafs Oldies. She had formed some really quite close friendships with women around her age and older from all parts of the world. She had found herself flying out to gigs in Italy, Holland and Norway meeting and sometimes staying with her new-found friends. To have the opportunity to stay in family homes in different countries was fantastic – and all because of a shared love for a young pop star. Many times either during their forum chats or through the hours that they spent queuing outside of venues they would reflect on this unexpected change of direction in their lives.

Janey had been perfectly content with her life and

wasn't aware that she was missing anything before she had discovered Adam. Now it was safe to say that her life pretty much revolved around him. All her annual leave days were allocated to gigs. Her colleagues knew that if she said that she was going to Milan for instance, it was a pretty safe bet that Adam Olsen was playing there. She spent all of her spare time either on OAFS or on travel or hotel websites. Sometimes she wondered how she had filled her time before Adam had entered her life.

They tried to find hotels that were within walking distance of the venues. By the time they had waited for Adam to come out after the gigs, public transport had usually stopped. They were always budget-conscious so tried to avoid having to use taxis.

Goodness knows how they would have managed all of this without the aid of the internet but as it was it was relatively easy. To be honest she was very surprised that Adam still came out to meet the fans after the gigs. He was incredibly generous with his time. She had assumed that as his popularity, and fame, grew he would become more distant and unobtainable. Not that she personally had had very much of his time of course. Right from that very first gig in Manchester it seemed that she was destined to always get a bum deal. She wasn't an outgoing gregarious character and when there was that level of competition for Adam's attention wallflowers weren't ever going to get a look in. Invariably she was pushed to a side whilst others dominated the conversation and his attention. It was the story of her life, but it didn't make it any easier to bear.

Vara seemed to consider herself Adam's best friend. She never stopped posting *Adam said this* or *Adam did that* and although Janey wasn't by nature an envious or jealous person it was difficult sometimes to accept it. She would give *anything* just to have one conversation with him, let alone one every time she went to a gig. Sarah too seemed to get more than what Janey felt to be her fair share of Adam's attention. For some reason she seemed to have caught his fascination after the Manchester gig and from then on he seemed to make a point of almost looking out for her and saying hi.

Despite all of that however, Janey enjoyed her OAFS jaunts. It was such fun meeting up with everyone. They all loved Adam obviously but it had become much more than that. It was a real network of friends who had a great time when they got together. There was a nucleus of hardcore fans who managed to get to most of the gigs and then there were many others who were just as big fans but weren't able to get to so many shows. This meant that wherever Janey travelled she was meeting different people and enjoying new experiences.

Today she was sitting in a busy courtyard garden in a small, slightly dubious hotel near to Parc des Princes in the Paris suburbs waiting for the others to arrive. Even within the UK the fans were spread far and wide geographically. On the forum it was easy enough to communicate no matter where they all lived but when it came to the gigs, quite often it was easier to travel separately and meet at the hotels or venue. OAFS had gone totally mad as soon as the PDP concert had been announced. Those that were able to get there were beside themselves with excitement and those that had no chance were desperate to read the reports, see the videos and ultimately buy the DVD that would no doubt eventually be sold. To play a stadium concert so early on in an artist's career, after the release of just one album was a fantastic achievement and the fans were incredibly proud of Adam.

Janey became aware of the noise level rising and looked towards the hotel reception. Sure enough Vara and Sarah had just arrived. Janey left her seat and went to meet them. Full of tales of negotiating the Paris Metro without a word of French between them the pair were in high spirits. Janey showed them to the room that they were all sharing and they hurriedly changed. Anxious to get to the venue as quickly as they could they were soon out of the hotel and, *multimap* print out in hand, they headed down Rue de Civry towards Parc des Princes.

As they approached the stadium they heard Adam's music. At first they thought it was pre-recorded but as they got closer they became aware that it was the sound check. They could see some fans pushing up against the fencing at one point and realised that it was possible to see in-between the stands into the stadium. They joined the small crowd and peered through the gap. All they could see however was the pitch which had been covered over, and the empty stands. But they could hear. Adams incredible vocals were soaring out for the whole neighbourhood to enjoy. When it became obvious that they couldn't see anything Janey turned around to take in the surrounding area. She gasped. The road running adjacent to the stadium had been closed and a zigzag fencing system had been erected right down the road. Fans were sitting, in the blazing sun, within the barriers and the queue extended as far as she could see. Cursing the fact that their travel arrangements had meant that they couldn't get there any earlier they hurried to find the end of the line.

*

Adam kept walking. He was determined he wasn't going to look behind him. He was striding down the middle of the covered pitch heading towards the far end of the stadium. He didn't want to turn around and see the stage until he got right to the back. He wanted to see what impact it would have from that distance. He reached the end and swung round. The big screens on either side of the stage were on and were showing the band. The set was illuminated as it would be later tonight as darkness started to descend. The stage was encased within a huge 'A'. Adam watched as thousands of tiny lights, starting at the base of the letter and working their way up brought the giant initial to life. When it was fully illuminated it flashed it's full stunning image a couple of times before going black then starting to repeat it's pattern from the bottom again.

Adam grinned. He had conceived this idea whilst messing around on a computer programme months ago and had managed to convince the set designer of it's worth. This gig was costing him a fortune. Yes, it was a sell out, but the expense of staging it would far outweigh the income. But Adam didn't care. He wanted to celebrate his success and thank everyone that had shown faith and supported him this far. He looked around the stadium. From this position it looked enormous. Adam looked at the stands and tried to imagine them full. He looked at the pitch area stretching out before him and pictured it covered in people. He had no doubts that they would come. The tickets were sold and a good percentage of the fans were already queued up in the road outside.

Everything was ready. Was he ready? He should be. He had been preparing and planning for this day for months. He had held countless meetings, rehearsed tirelessly, done everything that was humanly possible to try and guarantee that tonight was an amazing experience for everyone, but he felt an almost crushing sense of responsibility. So many people were relying on him. Fifty five thousand tickets sold. He swallowed hard. No matter how many times he thought it or said it, it didn't seem to become any easier to comprehend. 55,000 people wanting to come to listen to *him*. How had that happened?

Jason caught up with Adam and joined him in surveying the scene. The sound check had gone to plan and at this point everything was looking good. Adam grinned at him and Jason smiled back. Adam was handling stardom brilliantly. He was confident but remained grounded and he honestly had the world at his feet. Today was a huge day for him and he appeared to be enjoying it. He was calm and appeared relaxed.

Jason couldn't have asked for more. He would be glad when it was all over but he had confidence that Adam would pull it off.

5:00pm and the stadium gates opened. The first 1,000 fans in the queue had been given wristbands to allow them entry into the *golden circle* in front of the stage. Much to their huge relief Sarah, Vara and Janey had been within that 1,000 and as soon as their tickets were scanned they ran. As they headed down the pitch they shouted to each other trying to decide where to head. The front row had not surprisingly already been taken. There was a catwalk sticking out from the stage. The decision they had to make was whether to go to the end of the catwalk, where they felt certain Adam would spend quite a lot of time, or be on the second or third row in front of the main stage. They dithered, what should they do? They settled on the catwalk option.

Once in position they caught their breath and looked around them. This place was *huge*. They had watched with pride as the venues that Adam played got larger and larger but they had never envisaged that he would be playing a stadium so soon. They felt *so* proud of him. They had seen the membership of OAFS grow and grow on a daily basis and they felt proud that they had been there from the beginning. They loved the fact that Adam really appreciated his fans and always made the time to meet them when he could. But above all they loved Adam. They felt privileged to be fans of someone so amazingly talented who produced incredible music, was a fantastic live performer and on top of all that was a sensitive, caring guy.

They stood there now in the sun and contemplated their wait. Adam was due on stage at 9:00pm. Another four hours. The sun was still hot and there was no shade. There was no way they were going to shift from their positions so they would just have to cope. As the evening drew on they watched the stadium begin to fill up. The pitch area became fuller and the blue plastic seats in the stands started to apparently change colour as they filled.

Vara leant on Sarah. She was shattered. It had been a long day and she was never very good in the sun. But it wouldn't be too much longer now and the wait would be worth it. She couldn't *wait* to see Adam again. It was six months since she had last seen him and it felt like forever. She had been counting the days until today. Just two hours left now. The support band would start shortly. But then after tonight it would all be over again and it would be another long wait until she got to see Adam again. It wasn't fair. She loved this guy. It was only natural that she wanted, *needed* to see him regularly.

9:00pm. The sun had disappeared behind the stands and the lights around the stage were illuminated. The support band had been and gone. The stadium was full. The crowd were buzzing. Periodically Mexican waves swept around the stands and across the pitch. Vara, Sarah and Janey were about ready to explode with anticipation. Sarah kept looking at her watch. It was a nervous habit that manifested itself when she was anxious. She knew what time it was. She didn't need to keep looking. It was 9 o'clock and Adam would be on that huge stage any second now.

The backing track stopped suddenly and the band strode onto the stage. The loudest roar that Janey had ever heard filled the stadium. They played the first bars of Adam's opening track. All eyes were on the stage. Suddenly a trap door at the end of the catwalk opened up. Right in front of their eyes Adam rose magically before them. The big screens showed his image as he ascended. The huge 'A' burst into life. Head bowed, black top hat on, he looked like a magical ringmaster. From her position Janey felt as though she was virtually underneath him. She was looking straight at him as he held his head in the bowed position. She looked directly into his face. He was looking at her! Her heart leapt as the realisation hit her that he was indeed looking directly at *her*. 55,000 people in that stadium and he was looking at *her!* Adam lifted his head just as the band changed tempo, the timing was perfect. He leapt into the air and as he landed he started singing.

Sarah couldn't remember when she had enjoyed anything so much. For two hours Adam worked relentlessly. He moved up and down the catwalk and back and forth across the stage constantly. He never stopped moving. Sarah marveled at how he could sing so consistently well when he was running, dancing or jumping but somehow he did. As the sun gradually set over the Parc des Princes the sky displayed some incredible colours as day slipped into night. Within the stadium Adam Olsen provided some equally breathtaking moments for his adoring audience. Finally just before 11:30 after three encores and the knowledge that the curfew was rapidly approaching Adam took his last triumphant bow and ran off the stage for the final time.

*

Vara stuffed the Visa bill into the drawer in the dresser. She wasn't going to think about how many unpaid bills were in there. She *really* shouldn't have gone to PDP. There was no doubt about that. She was already in massive debt, mostly down to her going to a lot of gigs last year. She could never afford to pay more than the minimum amount off her Visa bill which meant that there was no hope of her ever making any headway on reducing what she owed. It was hopeless. But she couldn't *not* go to the gigs. She hadn't intended going to Paris. She had told herself that she needed to be strong. But when more and more OAFS signed up to go it became increasingly difficult to resist. It was Adam's first stadium gig after all. Her friends Sarah and Janey were going and it would be great fun. They would have such a laugh, and get to see Adam into the bargain. It was like a drug. She simply *couldn't* resist. They had certainly had fun. And the gig had been brilliant. Even now, almost a month later it still brought a smile to her face when she thought about it.

Adam just seemed to get better and better. He had taken the opportunity of the big concert to preview four songs from his forthcoming second album. She had immediately fallen in love with them and was now even more impatient for the album release date to be announced. Fortunately she had found videos on YouTube and had managed to get them onto her MP3 before the record company had got wise to them and had them removed. But she was still desperate to hear the full album and get proper studio versions.

But it was the memory of the meet and greet after the gig that brought the biggest smile to her face. They had waited what seemed like forever. They really weren't expecting Adam to come out afterwards. He must have been absolutely shattered after all. But frankly, if Adam was inside a building, they were going to wait outside, no matter how long they had to wait or how unlikely it seemed that he would come and meet them. It had been well past 1:00am before the car had finally pulled up the access ramp from underneath the stadium and approached the gates. They thought that the gates may just swing open and let the car out and that would be that, he would be gone. But no, just as the car cleared the gates it had stopped and Adam had got out. There weren't too many people waiting. Most of the thousands had headed straight off after the gig and would be safely home in their beds by now. But Adam had been determined to give the hundred or so that had persevered what they had waited for. Janey had smiled at him. That was all she ever seemed to do. Vara couldn't understand that. She knew, obviously, that some people were less confident or self-assured than others. But to be obsessed to the level that Janey was, to talk about and think about little else than Adam

24/7 and then not to be able to even utter *hello* was beyond Vara's comprehension. She and Sarah certainly hadn't been restrained. Adam knew them by now. They had been in the front row and waited outside enough venues by now for them to be very familiar faces to him.

'Hi, how are you? Good to see you again' he had greeted them, with a huge smile. Vara's heart was getting used to missing the odd beat now so it seemed to cope well. She had enthused about what an amazing show it was and Adam had seemed genuinely delighted that she had been pleased. She couldn't tell him of course that if he had sat on a stool in a church hall, with no fancy set or expensive trimmings she would have been equally satisfied. To be perfectly honest, he wouldn't even have needed to sing. She would be quite happy just to stand and gaze at him.

It was memories like that that made it all worthwhile. She walked away from the dreaded drawer that held all the bills. She would worry about that later. Maybe it would be a while before there were anymore gigs. She would have time to pay off a few bills before then. She made herself a coffee and sat at her computer. She opened up her pictures file and went into the PDP folder. Even though she hadn't taken many photos herself that night she had over 100 pictures in there. The OAFS were always very good at posting pictures on the website and she just saved them into her own files. There were quite a few from the meet and greet and she had saved any that showed Adam and her in the same shot. There he was, clearly smiling broadly directly at her. Vara sat back and sighed. But this time it wasn't a sigh of desperation over unpaid bills. It was a sigh of unadulterated bliss.

*

Sarah looked at the departure board. Ten minutes until her flight to Stansted was due to board. She had managed to work that morning and this mid-afternoon flight from Glasgow to London was perfect. An hour after takeoff she would be in London and heading towards the Roundhouse in Camden to meet the other OAFS. This gig had come out of the blue. It was one of those freebie things that you just sent your email address to and hoped for the best. Of course they had all applied for tickets but out of the OAFS membership only one or two had secured tickets via the traditional means through the promoter, although the AOFS admin team had managed to secure 100 tickets and had offered them on a first come first served basis on the website. The OAFS jungle telegraph had been in fine form that particular morning and within half an hour all the tickets had been allocated. All they needed to do was give their name at the venue, which would be checked off against the guest list.

Sarah settled into her seat on the plane, as much as it is possible to settle into a budget airline seat that is. She was excited about seeing Adam again, it was a while since she had seen him and withdrawal symptoms had definitely set in. But she was also nervous. She had made a decision and today she was hopefully going to implicate it. She shuddered a little with nervous excitement as she thought about it. She had decided that she wanted an Adam-related tattoo. She didn't have any tattoos and in some ways this decision surprised even her. However, having made up her mind she was determined that she was going to go through with it. Her thought processes had been through many designs including artwork from the album cover to Adam's name in block capitals and many things in between. One day she had been standing staring at the first thing that Adam had ever signed for her, her ticket after the Manchester gig. *To Sarah, love Adam O xx.* The thought suddenly struck her that she would love to have Adam's signature as her tattoo.

The more Sarah thought about it the more the idea grew on her. The trouble was, having made up her mind, she was desperate to implement her idea but she wasn't sure when her next opportunity to see Adam was going to arise. She could be waiting for months. Therefore she had been ecstatic when this gig had come along unexpectedly. She had, of course run the idea by Dan. He had been a little surprised but hadn't put up any opposition so she felt happy to go ahead with her plans. Confident that Adam would, as he usually did, come out to meet the fans after the gig she had gone ahead and made an appointment with a tattoo artist in her home town for the morning after the gig. Her plan was to ask Adam to sign her wrist after the gig then get it tattooed as soon as was possible. She hadn't shared her plans on the forum. She didn't want to run the risk of anyone else jumping in first and stealing her idea. But she *was* nervous about it. She would have much preferred it if there had been some way of pre-warning Adam what she was planning. She felt as if she was going to be putting him on the spot by asking him outright like that, without giving him time to think about it. However, after the gig was the only time fans were able to speak to Adam, and that was a lot more than fans of many artists got.

The Camden Roundhouse was an incredible venue. Originally a Victorian steam engine repair shed converted into a performing arts venue in 1964. Sarah could feel the history of the place as she stood on the spot that would have originally housed a railway turntable. As she stared up at the rafters she allowed her mind to picture some of the legendary performers who had played here: The Rolling Stones, Jimi Hendrix, Pink Floyd, David Bowie – and now, Adam Olsen. Sarah's face broke into a smile as she added Adam's name to her mental list of legends.

*

The gig was televised live which gave it an extra edge of excitement. The fans were as high as kites. Offering 100 tickets to the OAFS had been a good plan as it meant that the front row was occupied by real fanatics who weren't afraid of going crazy in front of the cameras. Adam had been on fire. Sarah loved it when he got TV exposure and he had certainly put on a great show tonight. It didn't matter how many times Sarah saw him, she could never get enough. Tonight she was particularly happy as Louise was here. Louise was a relatively new member of OAFS Oldies. She was also from Scotland and she and Sarah got on really well. Tonight she was doing a brilliant job of calming Sarah's nerves. After the gig they all wandered around to the back of the building. Then they went to the front. Then they went back to the rear. It was so difficult to know sometimes which entrance to wait at. The security staff couldn't always be trusted as they sometimes seemed to deliberately mislead them. With every change of their collective mind, Sarah got more and more nervous. And then suddenly, Adam was walking towards the group accompanied by Jason and the obligatory security guards. He started to make his way down the line. Sarah heard Louise asking him when he might be in Scotland then it was her turn.

'Hi Adam, please would you sign my arm so that I can get it tattooed?' There, it was out now, she had said it. Adam stared at her. He actually seemed to recoil slightly. She had certainly taken him by surprise, he looked quite shocked. 'It's ok if you don't want to do it,' she said. He was still looking at her intently. 'But I would really like you to.' He continued to look at her as if she was a mad woman. 'Please,' she pleaded.

Without taking his eyes off her he moved forward slightly and took her proffered arm. He held it to steady it as he carefully wrote his name on her wrist, adding a small picture of a heart and finishing it with an X. Sarah was ecstatic. She watched as Vara had her usual animated conversation with Adam, at the expense of everyone who was standing either side of her as they couldn't get a word in edgeways. This of course included poor Janey who still had never really managed to do much more than smile at him. They then all made their way down behind the crowd, following Adam as he worked his way down the line towards the car waiting at the bottom of the hill.

That night Sarah lay on the floor of a Travelodge room. She only had a few hours before her early morning flight which would get her home in time for her appointment with the tattooist. She hadn't booked a place in the room but one of the regular Oldies had kindly brought her a duvet to lie on for the few hours that she would be there, but Sarah didn't sleep. The busy central London room was light enough for her to be able to see Adam's signature on her arm. She lay staring at it until Adam's gentle tones, set as her alarm call on her phone, told her that it was time to get up and head to the airport.

*

Clare snapped down the lid of her laptop. Adam looked up. He was reading a new book and had just reached a particularly gripping part so he didn't really want to be interrupted. However, Clare clearly wasn't happy.

'What's up?' he queried.

'Why did you sign that woman's arm so that she could get it tattooed?' Clare still made a point of reading OAFS after the gigs to see what the reaction of the fans had been. This time she had seen a thread, started by Sarah, detailing every minute detail of how she had asked Adam to sign her arm, complete with photos of him doing it, and photos of the finished tattoo. Sarah was clearly over the moon. And Clare was raging.

Adam took a deep breath and cast his mind back to the previous night. He *had* been taken by surprise by the request. He had seen articles about fans asking people like Paul McCartney to sign their bodies so that they could be tattooed but he hadn't expected it himself. He still had trouble adjusting to his new status and sometimes he was a bit taken aback at the lengths that some of the fans would go to.

'It's not a big deal,' he said now to Clare. She glared at him and looked as though she may explode. Clearly that hadn't been the right thing to say.

'It might not be a big deal to you but it obviously is to her,' she hurled back at him. 'I've just been reading a thread of two hundred posts discussing the matter.'

'Well, you know what they are like,' Adam countered 'they discuss ridiculous things until the cows come home'.

'I know. And most of it I let go over my head but I am not happy with this Adam. *I* don't even have your name tattooed on my arm and I am your girlfriend for God's sake.' Clare's temper wasn't cooling.

Adam stood up and walked across the room. 'Well, you could have if you wanted to,' he grinned, knowing full well that she wouldn't even consider such an action. 'I have told you, it's no big deal. It's a fan with a pop singers name on her arm. It's not unique. It happens a lot. If she is crazy enough to want to do that, who am I to stop her?'

'You didn't have to actually sign it,' Clare persisted 'you could have said no. I know she could have had your name tattooed on her arm anyway, but you didn't have to actually sign it.' Her voice was softer now and rather than cross she sounded genuinely upset. Adam looked at her and went to sit next to her on the sofa. She leant into him as he slipped his arm around her.

'I'm sorry,' he said 'I wouldn't have done it if I had known that it would upset you. Forget it Clare. It's nothing. By tomorrow they will be discussing how tight my trousers are again. You seem to cope ok with that,' he grinned.

It was true. Generally Clare was able to cope with whatever was thrown at her. When she tried to rationalise why she was ok with them discussing Adam in intimate detail she reasoned that it was because she was totally secure in her relationship with him. She was 100% confident that he was absolutely unwaveringly faithful to her and that she was the most important person in his life. That gave her a kind of sense of superiority which acted like a shield. No matter what she read she knew that it all meant nothing. They could profess their love for him, fantasise about sleeping with him, whatever. She was secure in her belief that he was a one-woman man. Maybe she had just been feeling vulnerable this evening. She wasn't sure. But the tattoo thing had un nerved her. Why had he added the heart and the X? The woman had only asked him to sign his name after all. It just seemed a little too personal for

Clare's liking. She closed her eyes and let herself snuggle into his strong body. His fresh clean scent filled her nostrils and she allowed herself to wallow in his unique odour. For the first time she admitted to herself how hard it really was to be a pop star's girlfriend. It was his job but it wasn't like an ordinary job which you could leave at the office door. Adam's job infringed on every single aspect of their life. It was impossible to lead a normal life. It certainly brought its benefits in financial terms but it was hard. But that was the life they had. There was no going back. She had no option. If she wanted Adam she had to accept that thousands of other people wanted him too.

*

Janey took a sip of her drink and looked at the menu. This was great. A gig day that didn't involve hours standing on a cold and usually wet pavement. Today she was with Melanie. Melanie was one of the most prolific posters on OAFS Oldies but she didn't get to many gigs. As she was a wheelchair-user, travelling was difficult. But today she had managed to get to London and Janey was delighted. She was accompanying Melanie into the gig which meant that they would be let in just before the general doors opened. Therefore they were able to spend their pre-gig time in the pub. Janey had already had two Bacardi's. She had no need to implement her self-imposed *no drinks on gig day* regime as she would have free access to the toilets. Normally, when she was crammed into the front row she wouldn't contemplate leaving her position to go to the bathroom.

Tonight was going to be very different. Ok, so she wouldn't be on the front row. But she usually was and she was very aware of the fact that for her, it was a choice. For Melanie it wasn't. Janey knew full well that Melanie would have given anything to have had the opportunity to be on the front row. But it just wasn't an option. Health & Safety regulations decreed that wheelchair-users remain in the designated areas. The facilities varied from venue to venue. Some were quite good with a decent view, but some were dreadful, being placed at the back of the auditoriums. But in all honesty, wherever they were, it wasn't like being on the front row. Janey counted her blessings regularly that she was able to get that close to Adam when he was performing. For Melanie it was a distant dream. But tonight Janey was determined to do her best to ensure that they were going to have a great night.

They chose their meals and Janey went to the bar to order. When she returned she found Melanie surrounded by OAFS. They had slipped out of the queue for a brief while to thaw out and use the pubs toilets. Janey was never happy with doing that. It was her opinion that if you were in a queue you should stay in it. She didn't want people to think she was queue-jumping and she couldn't bear the thought of losing her place. But anyway, it wasn't up to her what other people wanted to do and it was nice to see them. Vara was sitting with her arm around Melanie. Janey knew that Melanie was a huge support to Vara online. Melanie was like the backbone of OAFS. She spent a lot of time on the forum and was always ready to offer help, support or advice to anyone who needed it. It was great to see her here, enjoying their company in Real Life. Vara, Sarah and a few of the other Oldies sat at their table and had a drink before heading back to the cold, dark queue.

Melanie and Janey stayed where they were, in the warm pub, happily eating their dinner and drinking more Bacardi's. They took the opportunity to have a good chat about OAFS. The fan club had been running about two years now. What had begun as a happy, inclusive community was beginning to show cracks. In the early days they were all singing off the same hymn sheet, excited to be involved as they watched Adam grow and develop from a breakthrough artist to a more established performer. But as time went on jealousies and insecurities began to creep in and divisions in the membership arose. Janey found this really sad. A mild mannered, happy person by nature, she hated any form of conflict. She would have given anything to go back to the early days.

In those days everyone was happy to share their experiences and if anyone got any of Adam's attention everyone seemed happy to share in their delight. Every word was reported on OAFS. But it wasn't like that now. Some people had become very secretive which led to speculation over what they were being secretive about. Some of the fans who were unable to get to gigs were envious of those whom had met Adam multiple times and were now very familiar to him. Janey accepted that nothing ever remained static, that everything was destined to change and evolve but still, she yearned for the halcyon early days of OAFS. Now, sitting here in the warmth with Melanie, reminiscing about how exhilarating those days were was very therapeutic. Recalling how delighted they had all been to discover that they weren't alone, that others, just as old as them were equally besotted with Adam. Janey adored Melanie and was always delighted to see that she was online when she logged on. There wasn't much about Adam or OAFS that Melanie wasn't au fait with. It was a pleasure to be able to spend time with Melanie and in a way it was a relief to not be with some of the other, more high-maintenance OAFS.

They finished their last drink at around 6:30 and headed around the corner. Tonight's gig was at Brixton Academy. Janey loved going to all the different venues. She was really looking forward to seeing inside this one. The dome forming the entrance to the building was resplendent in green lights, illuminating it's otherwise unglamorous surroundings. She pushed Melanie's wheelchair alongside the queue, stopping to say hi to familiar faces as they progressed towards the front. Janey felt very smug that tonight she didn't have to stand out in the cold then run like a mad woman once inside the building. That was always the tricky bit as the security people threatened you with a fate worse than death (i.e., being put out of the gig) if you ran, but everybody always did. The trick was to walk very fast until they turned their attention to the next person – then run. Janey was perfecting the procedure to a fine art. But not tonight.

This evening they made their way up the ramp towards the main entrance and waited for the doors to be opened to allow them and the other disabled guests to enter. Once inside, they remained in the foyer whilst the security checks were undertaken. Janey saw Adam's manager, Jason, talking to the staff and just for one moment she allowed her mind to wander off in a flight of fantasy, imagining what would happen if she followed Jason backstage. In reality she knew that she wouldn't last two minutes without being detected, but it didn't stop her daydreaming. In her head she was already in Adam's dressing room, chatting casually to him. As if she would ever have the confidence to do that! She snapped back to reality when Melanie looked at her questioningly and she realised that they were in danger of being left behind as everyone else was moving towards the auditorium. Melanie grinned at her, well aware of where her friend's thoughts had been.

Janey had been right to be excited about this building. Large for an indoor, non-arena venue, it held just short of 5,000 people. The perimeter of the theatre gave the appearance of being outdoors with balconies and columns of ornate plasterwork. The stage was surrounded by a huge arch, which Janey had learnt was called a *proscenium arch*. She liked to think that all this gig-going was expanding her knowledge. It kind of helped her to justify her activities to herself.

Melanie and Janey got settled into their positions. There was a railing in front of them, wide enough to put things on so Janey went to the bar and got them more drinks. They then watched from their vantage point as the general doors opened and the fans poured into the space below them. There were the OAFS, Sarah, Vara,

Louise and lots of other familiar faces, all rushing to get the best spots. Just gone 7 o'clock. Adam wouldn't be on stage until 9 but Janey knew that they would stay rooted to those positions now until he had left the stage in approximately 4-hours time. She went to the toilet. Just because she could. She was really enjoying this. She hoped that Melanie was too. She seemed to be and when Janey asked her she certainly said that she was happy. But Janey just couldn't get away from the feelings of injustice, that it wasn't fair that Melanie, who was just as big a fan of Adam as any one of the other OAFS, couldn't be down there to experience being on the front row; to have the opportunity to gain eye contact with Adam and to really feel that he was singing to *her*.

They watched the place fill up, they sat through the support act. Janey wasn't getting any more tolerant towards support acts. They were a cross that had to be borne in her opinion. They watched the roadies clear away the support bands gear and get the set ready for Adam. They got more and more impatient. And then finally it was time. The lights went down and the audience erupted. Janey gained almost as much pleasure in watching the crowd as she did in watching Adam. She looked at him, picked out by a single spotlight, head bowed, just waiting, letting the excitement level reach a crescendo before raising his head, and she watched the crowd go wild.

The gig was going well. Adam was a born entertainer. Confident, flamboyant and supremely talented, he gave an almost flawless performance every time he went on stage. Janey kept looking at Melanie and was sure that she was having a great time. She heaved a sigh of relief and leant back in her chair contentedly just as she felt a tap on her shoulder. She turned and came face to face with a pretty, blond young girl. Janey knew immediately that it was Clare, Adam's girlfriend. Clare liked to keep herself to herself and not be in the limelight at all. She and Adam kept their private life as quiet as possible and were never seen in the trashy magazines out on the town, but all the OAFS knew who she was.

There was the inevitable jealousy and envy that her relationship with Adam was bound to generate amongst his fans. Janey kept out of any such conversations on the forum. Yes, she was besotted with Adam but she was mature enough to realise that he was a young guy who was just as entitled to a private life and a relationship as anyone else. It upset her to read some of the hurtful remarks that were aimed at Clare, almost always totally unfounded as none of the OAFS actually knew her or anything about her. But now, here was Clare, smiling warmly at Janey.

'Would you both like to meet Adam after the gig?' Clare asked, indicating towards Janey and Melanie. Janey glanced at Melanie who initially had been so engrossed in watching what was happening on stage that she hadn't noticed Clare's presence.

'Oh, yes please' they both gushed. Clare smiled and handed Melanie a backstage pass.

'Just stay here after the gig finishes' she said and with that disappeared as quietly as she had appeared.

Janey looked at Melanie. Her eyes were welling over with tears. Janey felt as though her heart was about to burst. She looked down at the OAFS on the front row and knew what they would give to be in Melanie's position now. To have the chance to have an unrushed chat with Adam, perhaps even a photograph with him. So much better than the situations outside the venues which, although they were grateful for, usually resembled a cattle market. But this was fair. This was compensation. Melanie didn't have the opportunity to be down there jumping, dancing and screaming on the front row, smiling at and being smiled back at by Adam. She didn't have the chance to travel to different gigs all over the place. This was her one chance and Janey was overjoyed at what was going to happen. She looked at the backstage pass in Melanie's hand and hugged her friend as tears streamed down both their faces. Janey couldn't describe the gratitude that she felt towards Adam at that point. He didn't have to do this. He must be shattered at the end of a gig and surely he must really just want to go home. But to Janey it proved that he was as compassionate as he was talented and that he understood some of the frustrations that having a disability must bring.

The gig ended in the usual euphoric manner. Adam ran off the stage for the final time leaving the audience buzzing. Janey looked at Melanie with nervous excitement. She was impressed at how calm Melanie appeared. She knew that inside her stomach was probably like a butterfly farm but it didn't show. They stayed in their positions, as Clare had said, and watched the hall slowly empty. Some of the OAFS wandered over, managing to not get expelled by security and joined them on the platform. They had heard the news that Melanie had been given a backstage pass and wanted to come and share her excitement.

However, as the hall gradually emptied Janey became worried. The other OAFS were still there and the security staff didn't seem in any hurry to ask them to leave. Janey didn't want anything to spoil Melanie's special moment. Her anxiousness increased when the staff explained what the procedure would be. Due to the nature of the building it wasn't practical for wheelchair- users to access the backstage area so Adam would come to the platform to meet them there. The other OAFS were ecstatic. They were going to get to meet Adam too. Janey's heart sank. This was supposed to be Melanie's moment. She would have loved to have had the confidence to point this out to the others. To explain that she felt that this was done for the benefit of those that simply didn't have the opportunities that the others had. But she knew that she would be wasting her breath. They were so hyped up that they simply wouldn't have listened to reason. If Vara was to get any higher she would soon be on the ceiling.

After what seemed like forever a door opened on the other side of the hall. Adam emerged with Jason and a couple of security guys. Janey caught her breath. She didn't take her eyes off him as he strode across the now empty auditorium. It seemed almost surreal. Less than an hour ago, he had been on that stage strutting his stuff in front of thousands of manic, screaming fans. Now here he was walking across the floor, chatting to Jason, like an ordinary, regular guy. That was something that Janey always struggled with. She had difficulty in relating the onstage larger than life persona to the real life Adam who seemed so completely different, so quiet, almost shy.

Adam had now reached the far end of the platform and was meeting the other disabled guests, all of whom had just one carer with them. Janey looked again at their group and felt embarrassed. She felt that the privilege had been abused. They watched as Adam worked his way through the others and finally he got to them. Vara jumped in immediately. She actually grabbed hold of Adam's arm and started to go on about what a fantastic gig it had been. Sarah then managed to butt in to the conversation and before long there was what appeared to be a jovial group discussion taking place about the gig. But the trouble was, it was all going on at standing height. It was, quite literally, going above Melanie's head. Janey felt helpless. She couldn't get a word in edgeways. She knew that Adam's time would be limited and she felt that it was all slipping away, he hadn't even looked at Melanie yet.

Finally Adam managed to extract himself from Vara's grip and greet Melanie. She was able to give him the gift that she had for him and asked him if she could possibly have a photograph with him. Much to Janey's delight he happily posed for a picture with Melanie. Janey heaved a huge sigh of relief. At least Melanie had a precious memento now. But it still left a bad taste in

Janey's mouth that Vara and Sarah had put themselves before Melanie and hogged Adam's time. Adam had gone now and they were being encouraged to leave the building by the security staff who no doubt wanted to get home themselves. Janey took the handles of Melanie's chair and silently pushed her back outside. Inwardly she was boiling, her mind going over and over what she considered to be a major injustice, but outwardly she was just the usual plain, sweet, submissive Janey.

*

Vara rushed through the open gate at the underground station. She picked her moment carefully and ascended the escalator immediately behind an old lady with a wheeled shopping trolley. She knew the old dear wouldn't be able to get through the automatic barriers and would go to the gate seeking assistance. Vara's plan was that if she was quick enough she could rush through the gate. Head down, not daring to look either side of her, she executed her plan.

It worked. She was now standing with her back to a wall around a corner a safe distance from Highbury and Islington station and had chance to catch her breath and allow her heartbeat to return to normal. She hung her head, looking absently at her feet. Tears filled her eyes and her red shoes became blurred as she stared at them. She was disgusted with herself. In the last couple of years she had allowed herself to become someone that quite frankly disgusted her. Her compulsion to see

Adam and go to as many gigs as she possibly could had taken over her life. All sense of reason seemed to have deserted her. Vara had gone from being a responsible young woman and caring mother to a lying, deceptive cheat. She owed so much money she didn't even know where to start adding it all up. She didn't want to. She borrowed from everyone that she possibly could. She had two credit cards which she had thousands of pounds of debt on. She avoided phone calls and daren't answer the door as it was always someone wanting money.

The worst thing about all of it was the effect that it was having on Daisy. Vara knew that she was irritable and short tempered most of the time. The only way she could console herself was to spend even more time on OAFS as it felt like a sanctuary to her, but that meant even less time for Daisy. The only consolation was that Vara's mum began stepping in. Realising that her granddaughter was becoming neglected, she often collected her from school and took her to her home for the night. Although it was a measure of her own inadequacies at least Daisy was being well fed and getting the care and attention that she needed. Vara was just getting so bogged down in her own money worries that she was unable to think rationally and she knew that she was far from being the ideal parent. But she just couldn't stop going to the gigs.

Whenever a date was announced, by fair means or foul, she managed to secure a ticket. Until her credit cards had reached their limits she just put them on there. But when that was no longer an option she asked other

OAFS to buy them for her, always promising to pay them back, but in reality having no hope of doing so. It was at this point that she had started to be more inventive about her travel arrangements too and in recent months had become pretty efficient at fare evasion.

When it came to accommodation, again, she had to play on the goodwill of others and often didn't pay her share of the room bill. She knew she was doing wrong and yet she just couldn't stop it. Eventually of course, goodwill would run out and she would no longer be able to rely on others bailing her out. She didn't even want to contemplate what would happen then.

She couldn't imagine a life without seeing Adam regularly. Her obsession for him just seemed to deepen more and more. He was at the forefront of her mind all the time: when she was at work, when she was at home, when she was travelling, even when she was sleeping, he dominated her dreams and not always in the ways that she would expect, but he was often just there as a character performing some mundane role. However her day dreams were a different matter. Here he didn't appear as a shopkeeper or random passerby. In her waking dreams he was always her lover. That was the secret world that she could retreat to when the real world got too difficult.

But today wasn't difficult. Not now anyway. The difficult bit was over and once again she was where she was happiest, on her way to a gig. Tonight Adam was playing at the Union Chapel, Islington. To be honest, the venues didn't really interest Vara. She wasn't bothered if it was large or small, if it had historical or architectural interest or not. She knew that some of the Oldies took great delight in seeing all the different venues but as long as Adam was there she didn't really care. But, she conceded as the impressive Victorian Gothic structure loomed into view, it was kind of different to be seeing Adam playing in a church.

She could see the OAFS now, standing in the queue, in the dark, in the rain. It didn't seem to matter how bad the weather was, nothing would deter them from standing outside of venues to ensure that they got a good place. Vara's mood, already lightening as she had managed to get here for free and without being caught elevated even higher as she joined her friends. Sarah, Janey and Louise all hugged her warmly. It was great to be back in their company and Vara felt safe and warm. For a few hours she wouldn't think about her problems she would just have a brilliant time.

Union Chapel was a small venue and the audience sat on the church pews. It was truly amazing to see Adam perform there, in front of the impressive altar, with a backdrop of beautiful stained glass windows. Even an atheist like Vara couldn't fail to be impressed by the surroundings. Adams voice soared to the heights of the ornate interior and Vara sat on her pew and was, as ever, spellbound.

They were used to standing around waiting outside for what seemed like hours but this time it actually *was* several hours before Adam finally emerged from the chapel. Apparently there had been a party. For the first time ever, the fans saw Adam inebriated. He had obviously had a great time and he was barely able to stand without Jason's support. The car was, as always, waiting for him and he didn't spend long with the fans, he wasn't in a fit state to do so. After a very brief and almost incomprehensible few words Jason bundled him into the car, closed the door and he was away. In the few moments the car door was open Vara observed that no one else was inside. Clare wasn't there. That was unusual.

The fans were disappointed. They had waited a very long time and it was late. They were frozen to the bone and they had barely had 30 seconds of Adam's presence. They knew he didn't owe it to them to be charming and attentive after every gig but they had become complacent and had come to expect it.

The group slowly, disconsolately, started to disperse. Not wanting any of the others to know that she didn't have any where to stay Vara told them that it would soon be time for her train and said her goodbyes. She hated this part. They had all become so close. She loved spending time with them and they didn't know at the moment when the next gig was going to be. It could be months before she saw them again. In Vara's rapidly crumbling world, she found it hard to cope with the insecurity of not knowing when she would next see Sarah and Janey again – and Adam.

As she finally tore herself away and started to wander wearily back to the main road the reality that she didn't know when she would next see Adam again sank in. The rain had started again and Vara found it difficult to imagine that it was possible to feel much lower. It was true that it wasn't very long until the first train of the morning, but she didn't have a ticket and hadn't at that stage figured out a plan of how to get back to Manchester.

She always made sure that her plans were in place as much as was possible to get *to* the gigs, because that was the vital part, but getting home was a different matter. She wandered back on to Compton Terrace and walked back in front of the Chapel. It didn't look as impressive now. All the lights had been turned off hours ago. There was nothing for it but to just keep walking. She would have to get to the station and try and work something out from there. She looked at her little map and headed in the general direction of Euston. It wasn't too far. Although it was late the streets were still busy. Takeaway food shops were still open. Vara was desperately hungry but she literally didn't have a penny on her. She continued to wander.

After a while she became increasing desperate to use the toilet. She hadn't been for ages and the rain wasn't helping. She started to look for somewhere that she could possible go. There didn't seem to be anywhere around now. Then she saw a hotel. It looked very posh. She looked down at herself, wondering if she would be allowed through the door. Despite the rain, she had been under an umbrella all of the time and she didn't think she looked too bad. She always made an effort on gig days to look her very best. She walked up to the doorman and greeted him with confidence.

'Good Evening'.

'Good Evening madam,' he replied. Vara grinned to herself. But this was Kings Cross. Even in fancy hotels she could imagine that the doorman saw all sorts. She strode with a boldness and self assurance that she didn't really feel through the foyer. Fortunately the reception staff were busy and she was able to head straight through. Her luck was in and she soon saw a door indicating it was the ladies toilet.

On her way out Vara decided not to rush. This was a beautiful place and she might as well spend a few minutes out of the rain in this tranquil environment. She wandered back on to the main corridor enjoying the thickness of the plush carpet under her feet. Now that she wasn't so preoccupied with needing to find a bathroom she could take a good look around her. She could hear soft music coming from a bar to her right. She looked in. It wasn't over-populated, but then it was very late. She presumed however that this bar probably stayed open all night. There were probably about 10 people in, mostly at tables alone. Vara wondered briefly what sort of people would spend all night drinking in a bar alone. Musing this question she was just turning away when she stopped dead. The guy in the corner, who had been sitting slumped over his glass had just raised his head. It was Adam!

There was absolutely no doubt about it. Although on one level she couldn't really believe what she was seeing, every sense in her body was telling her she was correct. She spent almost every waking moment thinking of this guy, she was hardly not going to recognise him. Slowly she walked over to him. He was so drunk that he didn't register that anyone was approaching his table and so she just sat down.

'Hi Adam.'

Adam looked at her. She knew that he was having trouble focusing. It was so strange to see him in such a state. Normally he was so self-composed. He concentrated hard. He had only ever seen Vara at gigs so it was difficult to place her out of context. Anyway, people often came up to him and said hello. They felt that they knew him although he usually didn't have a clue who they were. But yes, he *did* recognise this pretty girl. She was one of the crazy fans that were at nearly all of his gigs.

'Oh hi, sorry, I didn't recognise you, I have had quite a few to drink this evening,' the sentence was amazingly coherent. Even though Adam was still drinking he seemed to have regained a little bit of his composure and Vara gave him her best disarming smile.

'It's ok. Everyone needs to be able to relax once in a while.' She looked around although it was unnecessary, she knew he was alone 'Are you on your own?'

'Yes,' he replied but didn't offer any explanation 'would you like a drink?'

'Yes please,' replied Vara. She couldn't believe how well this was going. She must have dreamt of a situation like this a thousand times, but she never imagined that it would actually happen.

Adam raised his hand and called the barman over who asked Vara what she would like. When he returned with the vodka and Coke Adam told him to charge it to his room. Vara gulped. He was booked into a room. Suddenly her mind was in overdrive. She slowly sipped her drink. She hadn't eaten all day so she knew that she had to take the drink very steadily or else it would go straight to her head. If she wanted to make the most of this one-in-a-million chance encounter she would have to keep her wits about her. They started to talk about the gig and were soon chatting as if they had known each other for years.

Vara had no idea why Adam was booked into a hotel alone when he lived in London with his girlfriend. However, she wasn't going to let that bother her. Their conversation became more and more flirtatious. Vara, well aware that being the sober one she had the upper hand, led Adam down the path that she wanted him to take and by the time she was on her second drink she was resting her head on his shoulder. When she suggested that it as it was late they should maybe head back to his room for a rest he raised no argument. He calmly stood up, took Vara's hand and led her from the bar.

'Good Night Mr Olsen' called the barman. Adam smiled and waved farewell, completely oblivious to the fact that for the last half hour the barman had been surreptitiously taking pictures of them on his mobile phone.

Vara followed Adam into the room and locked the door securely behind them. She had no idea what circumstances had led to Adam spending the night here but she didn't want to run the risk of them being disturbed. This was her moment and she was going to make the most of it.

No sooner where they in the room than Vara was in

Adam's arms. She knew that she was taking advantage of him. She knew that she was doing wrong but nothing in this world was likely to stop her from doing what she had in mind. This was the stuff of fantasies. She had played this scenario over and over in her mind so many times that it seemed almost familiar. She kissed him passionately and delighted in his response. With her head spinning she gently manoeuvered herself, whilst never loosening her grip on him, to the bed. They fell entwined upon it. Knowing that he was very probably incapable of removing his clothes she started to unbutton his shirt.

Always dressed stylishly, his shirt was of soft purple silk and Vara had never felt anything as luxurious and she ran her fingers over it several times before helping him to ease it off. All the time she continued to devour his deep sensuous kisses. She knew that she would have to break away from him at some point if she wanted to remove her own clothes but she was very reluctant to do so. His hands were all over her and she never wanted this to end. But maybe Adam wasn't quite as out of it as she had imagined as he started to undress her. She readily complied and before long they were both completely naked. Eager to move things on and to ensure that she got what she wanted, Vara wasted no time. Pushing Adam softly on to his back she straddled him. Slowly she eased herself down until he was fully inside her. If Vara had ever had to give a description of heaven on earth this would have been it. Slowly she started to move up and down. She began to vary her movements and speed, delighting in the blissful look on Adam's face. She leant forward to greedily take more of his delectable kisses. She sat back again and he grabbed hold of her waist. As he bounced her up and down upon himself she looked intently at him. He was sweating profusely, just like he did on stage.

Usually towards the end of the gigs he would take his shirt off and the fans would get to see his bare chest. But she had never seen it like this. She placed her hands on his chest as it rose and fell as he grew nearer and nearer to climax. He increased his grip on her waist. He was doing all the work now all she had to do was enjoy it. She had never enjoyed anything so much in her life. His breathing was becoming more and more rapid and then his face contorted. His eyes closed as ecstasy took his body over. Allowing her body her own release Vara's eyes also closed and she threw her head back in pure bliss.

Vara lay in Adam's arms listening to his soft steady breathing. He had fallen asleep almost immediately after their steamy session had culminated. She wanted to stay there forever. She never wanted to lose the scent of him which was currently invading her senses. But she knew she couldn't. As much as she hated the idea, she knew that she would have to leave. She didn't want to stay there until Adam woke up. She didn't know what his mood would be but it certainly wouldn't be the same as it had been before he went to sleep when he wasn't in all honesty really aware of what he was doing. She didn't want any awkward silences, or worse. She wanted what had happened to remain in her mind as an incredible memory. Reluctantly she eased herself gently away from his body. Not that she needed to worry about disturbing him. It would almost certainly be several more hours before he even began to stir.

Vara didn't take a shower. She wanted Adam's scent to stay on her body forever. That wouldn't be possible of course but it could certainly stay there for the duration of today. She used the bathroom to freshen up, marveling at all the high quality toiletries. You didn't get things like that in the budget hotels that she and the OAFS were used to staying in. As she walked back into the bedroom her eyes fell upon Adam's clothes, lying in an untidy heap on the floor. They were too nice to leave in that state, she would just pick them up and lay them over a chair. She wanted the chance to enjoy touching his clothes one final time, not just because the fabric was so luxurious but also, just because they were his. She smoothed her hands over the soft silk of the purple shirt, checking the name of the designer on the label as she did so then bent to pick up his trousers. As she lifted them, a wallet and phone fell from the pockets.

Vara stared. The part of her that was still had a functioning conscience was telling her to replace them and leave the room as she had planned to do. But these days the other part of her seemed to always win out. This part of her seemed to have abandoned any idea of having a conscience. With that half of her prevailing she opened the wallet. She had never seen so much cash. Why Adam felt the need to carry quite so much money around with him she really couldn't imagine. However, she wasn't going to spend too much time thinking about it. Without feeling even the slightest twinge of guilt she took several £50 notes out of the wallet and quickly slipped them into her pocket. She then turned her attention to the phone. Her own phone was nowhere near as sophisticated as this one but it didn't matter. She didn't need to know much about it to enable her to do what she intended to do. Making sure that her own phone was on silent she quickly entered her own number onto the screen of Adams phone then set it to call. Within seconds Adam's number was displayed on her own phone as an incoming call. Perfect.

That was all she needed to do. The number was in her phone now, she could label it as *Adam* later. Replacing both the wallet and phone back into the trouser pockets she laid the trousers over the back of a chair. With one final, yearning look at Adam lying in the bed she walked quietly to the door and let herself out.

*

Clare sank back into the seat of the black cab. She couldn't remember ever feeling so exhausted. She remembered the old saying *it never rains but it pours* but she honestly had never experienced two days as busy as the last two had been. She hadn't been to bed for over 36-hours. It had always been destined to be a busy time, but she had no idea that it was going to turn out quite the way it did. She and Adam were moving house. They had been delighted to get a sale on the flat, but completion on their new place wasn't until next week. However, not wanting to jeopardise the sale of the flat, they agreed that they would just move into a hotel for a few days. Adam also had a gig on the day that they were due to move out but Clare was confident that she would be able to cope with everything and nothing would need to be cancelled or changed. She would supervise the removal firm taking their things into storage and drop the keys for the flat into the solicitors office for 12-noon. She would then check into the hotel and head up to Islington for Adam's gig at the Union Chapel. She had really been looking forward to the intimate venue and seeing Adam do an acoustic set.

To be honest, they didn't have an awful lot of stuff to be moved from the flat. It was such a tiny place there really wasn't much room for anything. The new house was much bigger. They were so excited about moving and had spent the last couple of months planning the decoration and looking out for interesting pieces of furniture. Through her tiredness Clare allowed herself a smile as she thought excitedly about moving in next week.

Yesterday, however hadn't gone to plan. She had made it as far as the solicitors but just as she was leaving their office her phone rang. It was her sister, Helen. She was expecting her first baby and her contractions had just started. She didn't have a partner and Clare had readily agreed to be with Helen throughout her labour and the birth of her baby. Helen's due date hadn't been for another two weeks and as it was a first baby no one had expected it to be early. However, babies don't always follow the script and this one had decided that it was time to be born.

Clare had immediately jumped into a cab and headed to Helen's home.

The following 24- hours had certainly opened Clare's eyes. Up until then she had held a fairly romanticised vision of childbirth. All that had been wiped away very quickly. She now realised why, in no uncertain terms, it was called labour. She had watched helplessly as Helen struggled and battled to bring her little daughter into the world. But it was worth it in the end. Baby Chloe was absolutely beautiful. She was *so* small. At -7-lbs the midwife said it was a good weight for a first baby but Clare had never seen a newborn before. She was mesmerised by the size of the perfect little hands and feet and when she held her she felt as though she was holding a precious porcelain doll. But when she cried Clare was amazed that a little scrap of humanity like that could make such a noise!

Clare's maternal instinct had certainly kicked in and now, as she travelled across London in the cab she allowed herself to imagine Adam and herself holding their own tiny baby, and bringing him or her home to their new house. She was so lucky. Unlike Helen she was in a rock solid relationship with a man she absolutely adored and who was as besotted with her as she was with him. They hadn't discussed having children yet in any serious way. But in their general conversations it was an unspoken given that their future would include children. But for now she would be there to help and support Helen as much as she could as well as moving in to the new house of course and getting everything sorted there. A busy time ahead.

Clare closed her eyes and dozed contently for the rest of the journey until the cab pulled up at the hotel.

Clare couldn't wait to see Adam. She had had little contact with him since she had rushed off from the solicitor's office yesterday lunchtime. She didn't even know how the gig had gone. She assumed it had all gone well and she knew there had been a party planned afterwards. She had been disappointed to miss out on it all but on this occasion her sister had needed her more than Adam. He would have been fine, she was sure of that.

Clare took the lift up to the fourth floor and hurried along the corridor. She hadn't made it here yesterday and she still had the case with her that she had been going to deliver yesterday lunchtime. She reached the room and let herself in. She walked into the room and stopped dead as she surveyed the scene. Although it was mid afternoon the curtains were still closed. Adams clothes were folded on a chair but his shoes, socks and underwear were strewn about the floor. Adam himself was lying on the bed. Awake, but looking dreadful. She rushed over to him.

'Adam, whatever's the matter? You look terrible,' Clare took hold of his hand, it felt hot. She looked round the room, located the mini-bar, uncapped a bottle of water and poured a glass, holding it to Adam's lips. Trying to shake off feelings of guilt for not phoning him to check on him she tried to find out what the problem was. She has visions of him lying in this bed all alone dreadfully ill and not even being able to summon help. Tears welled in her eyes. Finally, Adam spoke,

'It's ok. I'm ok Clare. I just had too much to drink last night. That's all. I'm not really ill.'

Clare sank down on the bed next to him. Relief swept over her. He was hung over. That was all. She could cope with that. He hardly ever drank. That was probably why it had all gone a bit wrong last night. It wouldn't take much to get him drunk. But it was a party, he would have been happy because of the house sale and he obviously had just had a few too many. Relief, happiness and extreme exhaustion engulfed Clare and without even bothering to get undressed she fell straight into a blissful sleep.

*

Sarah wandered down the street looking absently into the shop windows as she passed. She quite liked taking this route for her dog walk, there were plenty of things to look at. She wasn't a great shopper, in fact, she was a pain to go shopping with. *Shop till you drop* wasn't a term that could be used to describe her, well, not unless she was allowed to drop within an hour that is. But the family had moved house recently and they now lived within a small town which meant that the shops were on her doorstep.

Early morning strolls with the dog, whilst the shops were still closed and the streets were almost empty suited her very well. This morning she had been admiring some warm looking, furry boots in the window of a shoe shop. They would have come in handy the other night when she was standing outside the Union Chapel in Islington, waiting for Adam to come out. A waste of time that had been of course. They had stood there for a couple of hours and then he had come out and more or less headed straight for the car, drunk as a skunk. In her more charitable moments she supposed she couldn't hold it against him really. He was normally so generous with his time and was always incredibly tolerant and polite to the fans. Sometimes Sarah cringed when she heard some of the things that people said to him. She marveled at his patience and tolerance. She had never once witnessed him being rude or even impolite to anyone even when they were being excessively demanding of him.

For instance, some people seemed to think they had a right to have a photograph taken with him if they had stood outside waiting for him. If there were two hundred people there and he did that for everyone he would be there all night. But at Union Chapel, he wasn't the usual charming Adam. In a way it had been quite amusing to see him drunk. None of them had seen him like that before. He could barely string two words together. It had been somewhat annoying, given that they had waited so long and it was absolutely freezing, but in fairness, he didn't *have* to spend half an hour of his own time meeting fans after every gig. Instead of complaining on the odd occasion that he didn't do it, they should really be grateful that he normally did. But of course, that wasn't human nature. Particularly in today's *me! me! me!* society. Everybody wanted their little bit of Adam.

Sarah walked further down the street. This wasn't a large place with big high street stores, just a small seaside town with old fashioned shops. Butcher, bakers, Sarah hadn't actually *seen* a candlestick maker but she wouldn't have been surprised if there was one. But she liked the atmosphere here, it was kind of like living in the past, but it was easy enough to escape when she wanted to rejoin the real world. She walked past the newsagent – just about the only shop that was open at this hour. She rarely bought a newspaper but as she passed she glanced at the headlines.

Suddenly she stopped. One of the red tops on the stand had caught her eye. She looked again and she felt her body completely freeze. On the front page was a picture of Adam. But it wasn't *just* Adam. It was Adam and Vara!

Sarah looked closely. It had clearly been taken after the Union Chapel gig, she could tell by what he was wearing. Sarah felt as though the wind had just been knocked out of her sails. She felt weak. Her mind couldn't process what she was seeing. She couldn't make sense of the image that was before her eyes. It just couldn't be correct – and yet it must be, it was a *photograph*. Dropping the dog's lead she rummaged for some money in her jacket pocket and hurriedly bought the paper. Outside the shop she read the headline above the picture: *Golden Boy's Halo Slips!*

Adam had been big news again recently. He had continued to try to keep a low profile but as his popularity had soared he had become more and more desirable to the tabloid journalists. Any little snippet or even half snippet of information that they could glean about him was exploited to, and beyond, it's full potential. Somehow it had become public knowledge that he and Clare were moving house and there had been pictures of them shopping for items for their new home. It really annoyed Sarah that people made their living from taking pictures of someone carrying a table lamp out of a shop but that was life these days. No one seemed to be allowed a private life if they were well known. But through all of this Adam had managed to maintain his image of Mr Nice Guy. He was always with Clare and they seemed blissfully happy in each other's company. He didn't spend his time drinking with celebrities, being thrown out of night clubs or being pictured with mystery women. He wasn't typical paparazzi fodder. Until now.

Here was a picture of him, clearly smashed out of his brain with his hands all over a 'unknown' woman. In some ways Sarah wished that the woman *was* unknown to her. She might have felt slightly less sick if that had been the case. She read the text:

Chart topping Golden boy, Adam Olsen, showed his true colours on Friday night in a central London hotel. The mega talented, multi award winning singer had earlier played an intimate session at Islington's Union Chapel and later took the opportunity of being intimate once more. Olsen, who is currently moving to a luxury St John's Wood pad with his blond girlfriend, Clare Ross, was

clearly enjoying a rare night of freedom. He drank and
flirted with the pretty unknown brunette before the couple
left hand in hand. Olsen was believed to be staying at the
hotel in Kings Cross and he and the girl were seen heading
into a lift together.

It said 'more pictures inside' and Sarah hurriedly turned the page to see more photos of the pair of them: two more of them sitting in the bar and one as they walked out together hand in hand. Sarah leant back against the wall of the shop. She was barely aware of her dog sitting obediently at her feet watching the world go by during this unexpected break in his usual morning routine. She didn't know what to think. Her head was spinning. Confusion, betrayal, hurt, anger, bewilderment – so many emotions were jostling for position inside her head. She just couldn't make sense of what she was seeing.

Sarah didn't always trust the tabloids, not many people did, but there was no disputing the hard evidence of photographs. As if in a trance, She tucked the paper under her arm and walked back home with her mind replaying over and over the moment that she and Janey had said goodbye to Vara on Friday evening. Despite the older women's concern for her safety Vara had been insistent that she would be ok and that she could make her own way back to the station. Sarah hadn't been comfortable with letting her go off on her own but Vara was a very determined young woman and once her mind was made up there was little that anyone could do to change it. They had watched as she walked off down the street and turned the corner. What on earth had happened once she was out of their sight?

*

Clare held Chloe so closely to her that Helen was beginning to get a little concerned for her daughters safety. Gently she eased her sister's grip on the baby, ensuring that the sleeping child was able to breathe freely. Clare, unaware that she had been holding the little one so tightly apologised. It was just so reassuring to be able to cradle little Chloe in her arms. She knew that she was gaining just as much comfort from the action as the baby was, probably even more so. Chloe's needs were simple. Clare's were a whole lot more complicated. She couldn't really remember ever crying as much as she had cried today. Not even throughout her whole childhood. It was difficult to contemplate how completely her world had been rocked. Everything she had believed in, looked forward to, being excited by had just been cruelly taken away from her. She couldn't think past the end of today yet alone any further into the future.

They had been woken that morning by Adam's phone. Clare watched him stumble out of bed, reach for his trousers and fumble about in the pockets until he finally located it. She smiled as she watched. They had been in bed for hours. She had desperately needed to catch up on sleep after being with Helen during Chloe's birth and it seemed that Adam needed to recover too. Clare wasn't even sure what time it was.

Adam's phone conversation and been brief and he came back to bed.

'Who was that?' she enquired.

'Jason,' replied Adam 'he's coming over.'

'Why?' Clare was surprised. She could see no reason why Jason would be coming to the hotel early on a Sunday morning.

'I don't know really. He said there was something in one of the papers that we needed to see.'

Clare got up. She was still in her clothes. She flicked the kettle on and headed into the bathroom. She couldn't imagine what could be in the paper that was so vitally important that they needed to see it immediately. However, she trusted Jason's judgment implicitly and if he felt that they needed to see it then they needed to see it.

When Clare emerged from the bathroom, showered and in fresh clothes it was to find Adam sitting on the bed, ashen-faced with a tabloid newspaper on his knee. She looked around the room. No one else was there. 'Where's Jason?' she asked.

'He's downstairs. He wanted to leave us on our own for a while.' Adam didn't look good. Clare was becoming more confused and worried by the second.

'Clare,' started Adam 'I really don't know what to say,' he passed her the paper.

Clare looked at the graphic picture on the front page and almost involuntarily turned the page to see the other photographs on the inner page. She read the short passage. It didn't say much, it didn't need to. The pictures said it all. She went to sit on the bed and her legs gave way beneath her. She didn't say anything, she couldn't. She couldn't even really bring herself to look at Adam at that point. She had no idea how long they sat there. Finally, Adam broke the silence.

'I don't know what to say Clare, I really don't,' his voice sounded small and broken. 'All I can say, and I know that it is totally inadequate, is that I have absolutely no memory of this.' Clare didn't look up. She knew who the girl was. It was one of the mad crazy fans that seemed to be everywhere. She could never understand how they managed to get to so many gigs, near or far, some of them seemed to *always* be there. This girl was one of them.

'What do you mean you have no memory of it Adam? You must have. You can't just totally forget being with someone no matter *how* drunk you are,' speaking like this to Adam was something that was alien to her. In all of their time together they had barely had a cross word. The fracas they had had following the tattoo incident was probably as near to an argument as they had ever got.

'I know it sounds pathetic Clare, but I just don't remember,' he protested. 'I don't even remember getting back to the hotel. I just about remember leaving the venue and everything after that is a blur.'

'How convenient' snapped Clare, finally finding her feet. She walked to the other side of the room and turned back to look at him 'Did you sleep with her?' It hurt her to even say the words.

Adam hung his head. He was still sitting on the edge of the bed. He was wearing just his underpants.

He looked almost vulnerable but Clare could feel no compassion towards him at that moment. 'I don't know,' he finally mumbled.

She glared at him. He hung his head even lower. He couldn't bring himself to look at her.

'*You don't know!*' Clare's temper erupted.' How can you not know if you have slept with somebody or not?'

Adam finally raised his head. Tears were streaming down his cheeks. 'I can't honestly say Clare. I really can't remember. If I say no I might be lying.' His head dropped again. 'I just don't know.' He tried to think. How on earth could he possibly forget what had happened? He was in total turmoil as he desperately tried to juggle his confusion with rising anger at the realization that he had been set up.

Clare was also finding it difficult to sort her thoughts coherently. It was bad enough to even *think* about the possibility of Adam having slept with someone else but to listen to him denying the memory was ten times worse. She grabbed her bag. 'I'm going!' she snapped. 'I can't stay here.'

Adam leapt from the bed, suddenly animated.

'Wait,' he pleaded. 'Jason says that there are paps all over outside. You flying out of here in a hurry would give them just what they are looking for,' Clare sighed heavily. She wasn't feeling charitable in any way towards Adam right now and his reputation was the last thing she cared about. He had managed to ruin that himself in one lurid evening. But she really couldn't face the idea of her cab being chased down the road with flash bulbs being pressed up to the window. 'Jason

said to call him if we want to get out. He's downstairs.'
Adam picked up his phone and called Jason.

After asking Jason to come up to the room Adam placed his phone down and shut himself in the bathroom. Clare sat with her head in her hands. She was trying to be strong. She wasn't going to allow herself to cry. Not here. Not yet. She wasn't going to cry in front of Adam. She might end up in his arms and that was the last place she wanted to be right now. Trying to concentrate on anything other than the horrible mental images that were flooding her mind she absently picked up Adams phone. She started to play about with it when a thought suddenly struck her. Maybe there would be something on his phone that would answer her questions better than he seemed able, or willing, to do. She looked at the text messages sent and received. Nothing. She went to call log. Incoming calls, nothing. Then she checked the dialed numbers log. There was a number listed with no name. She checked the details, dialed in the early hours of Saturday morning. Clare's resolve not to cry was being tested to the absolute limit. She was sure that the total revulsion that she felt was the only thing that was holding back her tears.

There was a knock at the door. Clare opened the door and fell into Jason's arms. He managed to close the door behind him and held her close. He knew that she needed physical and mental support. But he wanted to get her out of the hotel as quickly as possible. He had arranged for a car to come to a back entrance. It should be there by now.

'Are you ready?' he asked. Still holding him tightly

she nodded. Jason scanned the room and saw Clare's coat. He picked it up and they swiftly left the room.

*

Jason's plan worked. He managed to arrange with the hotel staff that they could use the delivery access and the car had been able to get in without anyone suspecting. Within minutes Clare was on her way to Helen's. Sitting in the car watching the rainy streets speed by, her vision became blurred as the tears finally began to spill over. By the time the car pulled up outside the house she was inconsolable. Helen had answered the door and Clare had collapsed into her arms. In the space of 24-hours the tables had completely turned. Yesterday Clare had been Helen's lifeline. Now she needed her sister to hold *her* up.

*

Jason pressed the button and leaned back against the lift wall as the doors closed. Thankfully there was no one else in there and he closed his eyes as he was carried up to the fourth floor. He really could kick himself for what had happened on Friday night. He knew that he wasn't responsible for every aspect of Adam's life but he had definitely made the wrong call on this occasion. He was so used to Adam having Clare by his side keeping him grounded. The party at Union Chapel had been a good one and he himself had drunk more than usual. When he sent Adam off in the car he had presumed that his work was done for the night.

Hindsight is a wonderful thing and he realised now that Adam had been in a very vulnerable position. Jason shouldn't have just assumed that he would have taken himself straight up to his hotel room. Sitting alone in that bar, totally off his head, he was a sitting duck. They say that no publicity is bad publicity but Adam's whole career was built on the squeaky clean Mr Nice Guy image. It was what his fans expected of him. Well, most of them. Obviously not the ones that have it in mind to drag him off to bed at the first opportunity. And then there was Clare. It had broken Jason's heart seeing her this morning putting on such a brave face when he could see that her whole body was racked with pain.

Jason knocked on Adam's door and waited. Eventually the door opened. Jason entered and Adam closed the door. Jason had never seen him looking as dreadful as he did now. He hadn't got dressed. His eyes were bloodshot and had dark rings underneath them. He hadn't shaved, probably since Friday, Jason realised. His hair was lank and needed washing. He looked so far removed from his usually perfectly polished persona that it was almost impossible to comprehend. He stood there, with his back to the door, and looked at Jason. Tears were brimming over from his swollen red eyes. Jason raised his arms and embraced him. He held him for several minutes. Adam was more to Jason than just someone he worked with and today the older man was feeling his pain. Finally Jason eased Adam's grip on him and moved away. He crossed the room, encouraging Adam to put some clothes on whilst he made some tea. With Adam dressed they sat sipping tea looking at each other.

'What's the story Adam?' Jason finally asked. Adam's brow darkened.

'That's the problem,' he started 'well, part of the problem anyway. I really don't know. I honestly don't remember. I remember getting into the car in Islington, just. After that I just can't recall anything.'.

'Nothing at all?' Jason raised his eyebrows.

'No. Absolutely nothing,' Adam shook his head to emphasise his point.

'What have you told Clare?' Jason enquired. Adam's expression became even more pained. Quietly, almost whispering he mumbled,

'I told her that I couldn't remember.'

Jason covered his face with his hands. 'I can't imagine that that went down too well'.

Adam shook his head.

'Between us we have to decide on the best plan,' Jason said. 'you know what they say, *"today's news is tomorrow's fish and chip wrappings'* but today, you *are* hot news. They are literally swarming like flies down there.'

Adam gulped. He hated the paparazzi with a passion. They would be in their element. For almost 3-years he had felt as though they had been waiting for him to slip up. His private life was, to them, terminally boring. He never gave them anything to report on. Clare and him visiting furniture stores was as good as it got. He could just picture them down there, rubbing their grubby little hands together.

'What are you thinking?' Adam asked his manager. He was hoping that Jason had a plan because if he was relying on him to come up with anything helpful he would be sadly disappointed. He felt as though his brain was in meltdown.

'I think we need to get you away for a while,' Jason stated. 'You can't run away forever of course and you'll have to come back at some point but a few days breathing space might help – if nothing else it will give you and Clare some time.'

Adam felt a physical pain run through him at the mention of Clare's name. He closed his eyes. It was almost too painful to think about. He didn't even want to imagine what she was going through. They were *so* close. It was always him that she came to for comfort. He was always there for her. He would hold her in his arms and listen to her worries. But he wasn't there for her now. He had let her down in the worst way imaginable. He would have given his career and his success up in a heartbeat if it would mean that he could turn back the clock. He wanted to be able to go to sleep and wake up with Clare smiling beside him and realise that all of this was just a nightmare. A nightmare it certainly was, but there was going to be no magical solution.

'Where would I go?' he asked Jason.

'Nice,' Jason declared. 'You know that I have a place there. If we get you down there you can lie low for a while. Clare can join you if or when she feels ready. We have a radio interview scheduled for this week but nothing else. I don't want to pull out of the interview as that will only add fuel to the fire but we can re negotiate with them and do it on the phone.'

Adam's heart sank at the thought of having to do a radio interview, but he knew Jason was right. Pulling out would not be a wise move.

'OK. When can I go?'

Jason stood up and reached for his phone. 'I'll get onto it now.'

*

Janey put the phone down and picked up her coffee. She put it back down again. It was cold. She and Sarah must have been talking much longer than she realised. They didn't often communicate by phone. Usually they just chatted on OAFS. But today was different. Today the forum was in complete turmoil. Allegations and accusations were flying all over the site. The situation was so volatile, it had taken everybody by complete surprise and emotions were all over the place. As Sarah and Janey were friends with Vara the other members wouldn't leave them alone, convinced that they must have inside knowledge about the circumstances surrounding Friday night's events.

They had been bombarded with questions. 'What did they know?' 'How long had this been going on?' 'How could Vara be so deceitful' 'What about Clare'. One thing was clear. Clare, who until now had been the villain of the piece as far as most of Adam's fans were concerned had suddenly become someone to be pitied and Vara had become the most hated person on the forum. Trying not to get drawn into the increasingly heated debate too deeply Janey had suggested to Sarah that they talk on the phone.

Not that they were able to make much sense of it either. They were in agreement that there had been no outward signs as Vara left on Friday night that anything was different. On reflection they agreed that Vara had, of late, become slightly more guarded regarding her plans. They assumed that this was down to her money problems. But maybe not. Maybe she had been hiding something from them for some time. They felt hurt and betrayed.

Janey, Sarah and the other Oldies had taken Vara to their hearts. She was much younger than them but she had seemed to enjoy their company. When they got together at the gigs they had always had a great time. On the forum they had shared many laughs as well as supporting her when she needed it. Now they felt as though everything had been thrown back in their faces. They had visions of her meeting Adam for secret liaisons whilst still engaging in their *imagine if* type chats online. They felt sick at the thought of someone whom they had considered a friend laughing behind their backs. And they genuinely felt for Clare. Surely she was the innocent victim in all of this? She seemed such a nice girl. Her heart must be broken.

Then there was Adam. How could they even begin to process their thoughts and feelings towards him? They had spent the last almost three years totally besotted with him. They adored his music, respected his amazing talent as a musician and songwriter and had grown to love his as a person. Their lives had more or less revolved around him since they had discovered him. How would they feel about him now? Could they still look at him in the same way. Could he still be their golden boy? They didn't know.

Neither of them had heard from Vara. Janey hoped that this would continue to be the case for the foreseeable future. She couldn't imagine how she could begin to be civil to her at this stage. What did you say to someone who has turned your world upside down? Someone that you had considered to be a dear friend that had turned round and stabbed you in the back? Janey went to make herself another cup of coffee. She was having difficulty in imagining the way forward. On a personal level she didn't know where her emotions were going to take her as she tried to make sense of all of this. For Adam, she had no idea how this would affect his career.

Things like this weren't unusual in the world of pop music, but it was all new in the world of Adam Olsen. He was due to do a radio interview in a couple of days. She wondered if he would go ahead with it. She hoped he would and that he would take the opportunity to address the issue on-air. She couldn't imagine the interviewer would let him get away without mentioning it. But on the other hand she was scared to hear what he might say. She didn't want to hear it. Whatever the truth was she didn't really want to know. She would prefer to bury her head in the sand. She wanted to keep him as the magical Mr Perfect that he had always been in her little fantasy world. Tears stung her eyes. She felt silly in a way. Adam Olsen was a pop star after all. It wasn't as if her best friend had betrayed her by running off with her husband or anything.

But that was what it felt like. Having spent the day with her emotions in turmoil they finally got the better of her and she broke down. She cried until she couldn't cry any more. Adam and OAFS had become so important to her. Now everything had been turned upside down. She felt completely lost.

*

The wind whipped around Adams legs. He didn't really notice. He was wrapped up in his world of writing and was oblivious to his surroundings. Today he had written four songs. It was the only way he knew to try and sort out his feelings and emotions. Clare wasn't answering his calls and he could understand that. But he needed to talk to her. On Sunday morning he had been so shocked and confused that he had barely been able to string two words together. Although now he still didn't really have any clearer recollection of Friday night at least he felt that he would be able to discuss the situation if she would give him the opportunity. But he knew it was a big ask. He knew how much she would be hurting. He was hurting too but he realised that he only had himself to blame and in some ways that seemed worse.

Jason had reported that there had been nothing new

in the papers that morning. For that, Adam was hugely relieved. Maybe the story would just fade. He could live in hope. He had spent the day sitting on the terrace of Jason's apartment in Nice committing his inner confusion to paper. He now pushed his notebook away and looked at his watch. Four PM. He leaned back in his chair and for the first time that day, took in his surroundings. It was a pleasant terrace furnished simply with wrought iron table and chairs and it brought Adam back to the morning of his stadium gig in Paris when he and Clare had sat at a similar table, bathed in both early morning sunshine and their love for each other.

He closed his eyes. It hurt too much to think of times like that. What would he do if Clare wouldn't have him back? He couldn't contemplate a life without her. He didn't even want to think of his daily life without her by his side. He thought of their new house. They were due to get the keys this week. They had been so excited about it, neither of them could wait. It was going to be the first house that they had chosen together, their first *real* home. The flat really hadn't been big enough for the two of them and they had outgrown it long ago. But because they were so busy it had taken this long to get round to finding a new place. The house was very smart and they had chosen some beautiful things to furnish it with. Decorators were commissioned to go in as soon as they had received the keys. A break in Adam's schedule had been arranged so that they could both be around for a few weeks. Everything had been organised so perfectly and then he had managed to foul it all up with one night of reckless behaviour. He never wanted to touch alcohol again.

Adam's thoughts shifted to the girl, the *mystery woman* in the pictures with him. As much as he had tried he still couldn't remember much about their encounter. The pictures showed them in the bar and leaving it, so clearly that must have happened. Presumably they had indeed gone to his room. Like Clare he too found it fairly incomprehensible that one could forget having sex. But he also found it hard to believe that they hadn't, given the rather lurid photographs taken in the bar. So, like Clare and no doubt everyone else, he had to assume that they had. How could he? How could he have allowed himself to be lured into such a situation. He had been so incredibly stupid, it really was beyond belief.

He remembered the girl from the gigs. He couldn't recall her name but he had certainly seen her, and talked to her, on lots of occasions. She was at a lot of the gigs. He supposed in a way that she too was a victim in this. Yes, she had probably taken advantage of his vulnerability on Friday night but she couldn't be held responsible for the actions of whoever had taken those photographs. She had clearly been as oblivious to the camera as him. Someone had obviously seen the opportunity to make a few quid, probably quite a lot actually, and had seized the chance. *That* wasn't the girl's fault. She must have left the room at some point, thankfully long before Clare arrived, and as far as she was concerned that was the end of it. He assumed that she would have been as shocked as he was to see the pictures.

Tomorrow he had to do the radio interview. It was for the BBC with a presenter who had interviewed him a few times before. The booking had been made originally to publicise a concert that Adam was doing for charity. Jason had been in touch with the producers to rearrange that Adam would now partake in the interview by telephone instead of in person. He had acknowledged that there would be a public expectation to address the newspaper pictures but had stressed that the presenter was not to dwell on the subject.

Adam felt reasonably comfortable that the presenter wouldn't milk the situation too much. He would have liked to have spoken to Clare though before he spoke to the general public. He would like to speak to Clare more than anything. He stood up and went back inside, checking his phone again, just on the off chance that he had missed a message from Clare. Her lovely face smiled up at him as he looked at the screen, but it was just the screensaver. No new messages. Dejectedly he threw himself down onto the sofa. Never had he felt so helpless. During all the years that he was struggling to become recognised as a creditable singer/songwriter he had never felt like this. Yes sometimes, quite often, he felt miserable, downhearted and sometimes rejected, but he never felt like this. Back then he always had faith. He believed that he could do it, that eventually his talent would win through and the world would believe in him. Now he didn't even believe in himself. Why would anyone else want to believe in him? He had ruined everything.

*

The figure looked enormous. Vara looked at it again to make sure that she had written it down correctly. She had. There was no question about it. This was a six figure sum. She had had no hesitation in contacting the newspaper to tell them that she was the mystery woman in the pictures with Adam Olsen. She knew that they would be willing to pay a lot of money for her story but she hadn't realised quite how much. She was in shock. Never in her life had she imagined that she would ever get her hands on that sort of money. It was beyond her comprehension. She felt no guilt. Why should she? The pictures were already out there, it wasn't as if she was exposing anything. The story had already been written she was just going to fill in the facts. It wasn't her that had sold the photos to the paper. She had no idea that someone had taken pictures, it had come as a complete surprise to her. She had logged onto OAFS on Sunday morning as she usually did and been completely shocked. She hadn't posted on the site. In fact she had logged off almost immediately so that her name didn't show on the members online list and had logged back in as a guest so that she could read without being detected.

Vara knew she wasn't going to be Miss Popular on there. But really, what did that matter? Life wasn't a popularity contest after all. It was about surviving and to survive you needed money. She seemed to have been presented, quite unexpectedly, with an opportunity to solve all of her problems and to give Daisy and herself a better life. Who wouldn't grab an opportunity like that? She had gone out and spent some of the money that she had left after raiding Adam's wallet and bought a copy of the paper. She had found the number for the news desk and had dialed it with no hesitation. After answering various questions to validate that she was indeed who she said she was they made her an offer subject to final verification. She had to agree be interviewed in person so that they could ensure that she matched the girl in the pictures. She had no problem with that.

Vara quite relished the thought of having the opportunity to talk about her night with Adam. An appointment had been made for her to meet with a reporter and photographer in Manchester city centre. They didn't seem to have a problem with travelling up from London to interview her. She felt like a celebrity. She couldn't believe how her fortunes had changed in 36-hours. On Friday night she was traipsing the cold, rainy streets of London without a penny to her name. Now she was front page news and was about to be paid more money than she could ever have contemplated having. Funny old world.

She hadn't collected Daisy back from her mother's house yet so she might as well leave her there. She didn't want to have to worry about Daisy when she was going to meet the journalists. She had a shower and did her hair. If she set off now she would probably have time to call and get a new outfit before the meeting. Then she would look her absolute best. Maybe she could even get one of those free makeovers that they do in the department stores when they are trying to sell you make-up. She was going to enjoy this. Her plan in place, Vara wasted no more time and rushed off to the shower.

Having clarified her identity and confirmed terms of payment the interview began. Vara left no stone unturned in her account of Friday evening's events. Unlike Adam, she was in no doubt about what had happened. She described in detail how she had attended the gig in Islington and had later come across Adam by chance in the hotel bar. As she was already familiar with him, being a huge fan, she had had no hesitation in approaching him. He had bought her a couple of drinks, they had gone up to his room and they had had sex. The journalist questioned how, if Adam had been as drunk as he appeared in the pictures they had managed to have sex. Vara had confirmed that he had been very capable indeed. Vara said that afterwards she had left the room and hadn't heard from Adam since.

All together the interview probably took about an hour. She then posed for photographs, collected her payment and left. The journalists stayed where they were, busy at their laptops, ensuring that the story and pictures made the deadline for tomorrow morning's paper. Happy with the content, they submitted their work. They would be on the front page tomorrow.

*

The interview was due to air around 11:15am. It was live. The presenter had already confirmed that it would be via the telephone. Clare was surprised. She had set it up several weeks ago and it was definitely supposed to be live from the studio.

'Coward,' was her first thought. Adam obviously couldn't face walking through a crowd of journalists and probably some fans too if they knew he was due at the BBC. She had spent the first two days crying almost non-stop. Helen had been unable to convince her to eat anything and all she had managed to do was drink endless tea.

By the end of Monday she had started to pull herself together. After all, it wasn't fair on Helen. She had just given birth, the last thing that Clare should be being was a burden to her sister. On Monday evening whilst Helen had been feeding Chloe, Clare had managed to cook a meal for the two of them. Chloe had then very accommodatingly slept whilst they sat down together and ate.

Clare missed Adam like crazy. He was her whole life. Particularly since they had been working together there was very little that she did that didn't involve Adam. Their working life was so very public that in their private life they didn't really tend to mix much with other people. She had more or less lost touch with most of her own friends; she simply didn't have time to keep up with them. Therefore, to be suddenly thrown into a life without Adam was almost unbearable. Being with Helen and Chloe was a blessing in a way. Life with a brand new baby was far from easy and she was glad that she was here for Helen. It had never occurred to her that her sister was going to need her after the birth and she was glad to be able to help. As long as she could keep from crying that was. She did miss Adam, so much that it hurt, and yet she couldn't forgive him. She couldn't even bring herself to talk to him. He was leaving multiple messages on her phone but she just couldn't do it. Not yet. She wondered where he was. She doubted that he was still at the hotel. That would be madness with the press camped out at the door. He couldn't be at home. They didn't currently have a home. Perhaps he was at Jason's.

It was 11:00am and almost time for the interview. Clare wondered what would be going through Adam's mind. He was normally supremely confident and something like this would have just been routine. But this morning's papers had opened up the whole dirty business again. The girl had sold her story. The revelation so-called hadn't really affected Clare too much because it was nothing she didn't already know. She had been in no doubt right from the beginning that Adam had had sex with her even if he hadn't confirmed it. In some ways, reading that it had been a chance encounter and not something that had been planned or pre meditated had been kind of reassuring. Clearly Adam had been drunk out of his mind and it had become clear to Clare that he had been taken advantage of. That didn't excuse it but it made more sense than any of the other possible scenarios that had been pounding through her head since Sunday morning.

11:15am. The presenter introduced Adam and she heard him say good morning. Her heart skipped a beat.

Hearing his voice was both painful and pleasant at the same time if that was possible. The interviewer didn't waste any time in tackling the issue. He asked Adam to give his side of the story as Vara Reid, as everyone now knew she was called, had obviously wasted no time in giving hers. Adam started to speak in a calm, measured voice. He said that he was extremely disappointed in himself. He couldn't deny what had happened but wanted to say that it was in no way planned. He didn't want to use the word victim as he clearly should have been capable of looking after himself but he felt that he had been caught in a very vulnerable state. His voice was beginning to crack a little bit now and Clare felt her heart start to go out to him. She looked across the table at Helen who was quietly feeding Chloe. Helen gave Clare a small, encouraging smile. Adam's voice continued to fill the small kitchen.

'I think it would be impossible for me to feel worse about myself than I feel right now,' he said. 'I have let myself down, I have let my fans down and most importantly I have let my beautiful girlfriend, Clare, down. I have broken her heart and in doing so I have also broken my own.' Clare felt that she could almost hear a sob in his voice as he finished speaking. The interviewer jumped in and said that they would play one of Adam's tracks. As his melodic vocals filled the air Clare felt her broken heart start to melt. She picked up her phone and dialed Jason's number. He answered immediately.

'Where's Adam?' she asked.

'Nice'.

'Book me a flight please.'

She didn't listen to the rest of the interview.

*

The Cote d'Azur was aptly named. Even now, in early March the Mediterranean was the most incredible blue, shimmering in the weak, late afternoon sun. Adam sat outside the beach front bar, idly sipping his coffee and staring out to sea. Also at the table was Steve, a bodyguard who Jason employed sometimes to look after Adam. Mostly at the gigs when he knew there would be a lot of fans around but at various other times too. It was a shame that he hadn't been on duty last Friday night; they could all see that now, after the event. But, once bitten twice shy, Jason wasn't taking any chances. He had sent Steve down to Nice with Adam. Adam was huge in France and although Jason thought that he probably wouldn't stray far from the apartment, he had erred on the side of caution. Steve's eyes continuously scanned the surrounding area.

Although giving the appearance of looking out to sea, Adam was deep in thought. The interview seemed to have gone well enough this morning. He had had time to recover himself whilst his single had been played and afterwards he was able to talk about the upcoming charity concert in a calm manner. He knew that he would probably get slated in some corners for being over sentimental and using the air waves to try and win back public favour. But that hadn't been his intention. He had spoken from the heart. You can never please all of the people all of the time and it would be crazy to even try.

He wondered if Clare had been listening. If she had, he wondered what her reaction had been. He so wanted to talk to her. He had tried her phone immediately after the interview and had been a little put out to find it was engaged. Did that mean she hadn't even been listening to the radio when he was on? He had tried again about an hour later but she didn't answer. It was really beginning to get him down. How long was she going to keep this up? They would have to talk eventually, even if it was only over practicalities. But he desperately hoped that wouldn't be the case. He hoped more than anything that they could be reconciled, and soon.

As the taxi swung around the corner Clare saw Adam sitting at the table outside the bar. He was wrapped up in a warm, dark blue wool jacket with a cashmere hat and scarf with his hands wrapped around a coffee cup. She only got a quick glimpse of him but it was enough to make her heart leap. He looked like a lost little boy. She couldn't wait to surprise him. She knew that Steve had spotted her in the taxi. She had asked Jason not to tell Adam of her impending arrival but she knew that Steve knew. He had managed a quick grin as the cab passed by. The apartment was 50-meters away from the bar. Jason had given her a spare key so she rushed in, dumped her bag and headed straight back out again.

Adam didn't see her coming. He was still staring vacantly out to sea, his hand wrapped around a now stone cold cup. Approaching from the side he was still totally unaware of her presence until the moment that she leant forward and gently kissed his forehead. Snapping into life he leapt from his chair.

'Clare!!!' He grabbed hold of her and held her so tightly that she could barely breath. Finally easing his grip, he held her at arm's length and looked straight into her eyes.

'I am *so* sorry Clare' he said.

She nodded. 'I know you are Adam.'

They went back to the apartment. But they didn't really want to be there. They didn't want to be in Nice. They wanted to be in London, in their new house. Together.

The next morning they flew home.

*

The playpark was busy. The weather was beginning to pick up now and people were making the most of it. Vara sat on the bench playing with her new phone, occasionally looking up to make sure that Daisy was ok. She was fine. She had met one of her school friends and they were having fun on the climbing-frame. Vara sighed contentedly. She had been able to be a much better mum since she had been paid all that money from the newspaper. In the aftermath of the article there had been one or two other offers from trashy magazines, which she had grabbed with both hands, she might as well make the most of it. But the paps soon realised that there were no legs to the story – it wasn't going to run and run. It was a one-off and interest in her had faded by the second week. Her mother had been absolutely appalled by her behaviour and for the two weeks that she was a tabloid minor celebrity she had insisted on keeping Daisy at her home and away from what she saw as adverse publicity. But things had settled now and Vara and her mother had made an uneasy truce. Vara had been able to cut her hours at work a little and so she could spend more time with Daisy. The other big change in her life was that she didn't spend hours on OAFS anymore. That had been the hard part. The forum had become so important to her over the last three years and she had lost that element of her social life overnight. She knew that she wouldn't be welcome there so she decided to cut all links. She still logged in as a guest so that she could see if there were any gigs coming up or anything else of importance but she never logged in under her user name.

It had been hard to lose the friendship of the Oldies. She missed her online chats with Melanie. How she would have loved to have been able to pour her heart out about how isolated she felt now. But she was wise enough to realise that that was a no-hoper. She wasn't going to win any sympathy on OAFS for the predicament that she now found herself in. Then there were the gigs. Adam had a charity gig coming up. How great it had been to be able to buy her own ticket without having to borrow money. But she was more than a little worried about the reaction that she would get from her former friends. She hadn't dared contact Janey or Sarah since Union Chapel. She knew that they would both be at the charity gig. It was going to be impossible to avoid them. But she couldn't contemplate *not* going. She was *desperate* to see Adam again. She had relived their night together over and over in her head so many times. Sometimes she almost couldn't believe that it had happened but she knew it had. Then of course there was the other thing. The thing that she was getting increasingly excited about as each day passed.

Vara thought that she was pregnant. She found the prospect so exciting she hardly dare begin to believe it. The possibility hadn't even occurred to her at first. She was just so high about having spent a night with Adam that she couldn't really see beyond that initially. Then the whole thing regarding the media took over her thoughts for a couple of weeks. However, she had been pregnant before of course so she knew the signs. She couldn't believe her luck. She always hoped that she would be able to give Daisy a brother or sister one day. She had split up with Daisy's father before her daughter was even born. They had both been very young, just teenagers and when Vara discovered she was pregnant he quickly lost interest. Her experience of parenthood began the hard way, with her feeling lonely and rejected. Her first choice now would have been to have had a second child as part of a stable, loving relationship but she had learnt that you can't have everything you want in this world. If she had thought of a second choice ideal situation, having Adam's baby with enough money to not have to worry about finances would definitely have been her chosen option.

She now sat staring at Adam's number. As soon as the money had cleared from the newspaper payment she had gone out and bought an identical phone to Adam's. She loved the fact that they had the same phone *and* she had his number. She never called, but she looked at it all the time. It gave her great comfort just to see it there, first on the list. She knew that it was simply a fact that alphabetically Adam was going to be the first on her list of contacts, but somehow it seemed more significant than just being a plain simple boring fact. It just felt *right*. But she would need to ring it soon. She would leave it a few more days. Then she would get a pregnancy testing kit just to be sure. But she was pretty certain really. She was pregnant with Adam's baby and she was going to tell him.

Vara called Daisy over. It was beginning to get cooler now and it was time to go home. Reluctantly Daisy bid her friend goodbye and wandered back to her mum. She didn't want to leave her friend and the park but maybe they would stop at McDonald's on the way home. They had a car now and mum was a lot more fun to be with again. She spent much less time on the computer and she was always taking her out and about. Sometimes they went shopping and bought cool things or sometimes they went on outings. Daisy's bedroom was going to be redecorated and mum had bought her lots of new toys – and it wasn't even her birthday or Christmas. Daisy didn't understand what had happened to cause all these changes. She knew it had something to do with Adam Olsen and some of the older children at school had said some cruel things to her about her mum. She didn't really understand some of the words they had used and the teachers had told the other children off. But whatever it was, it couldn't really be a bad thing could it? Not if it meant that they suddenly had a lot more money and were able to do exciting things.

Vara started up the car. She had learnt to drive when she was seventeen but had never been able to afford a car of her own before. After her new phone it had been the first thing she had bought. A brand new, bright red VW Beetle. It was perfect. She felt that it really suited her personality. She had also splashed out on a personalised number plate V84 ARA. Her name and year of birth. She had been delighted to find that plate was available. She had bought a coordinating booster seat for Daisy and now she was almost certainly going to be buying a baby seat too. Ok, so she wasn't the most popular person amongst the school mums. Her own mother was disgusted with her and she had lost of lot of the friends that she had been close to. But she had a new car, a top of the range phone, designer clothes and was expecting the baby of one of the country's top pop stars. What more could a girl ask for?

*

'Adam!' Clare called upstairs. They were still trying to get used to the scale of the new house. She only wanted to tell him that the coffee was ready but if she was downstairs and he was on the top floor it was really difficult to make herself heard. It was so very different from the flat. There were only four rooms in total there, all on the same floor. It was impossible for either of them *not* to know exactly what the other one was doing. She loved the new house. It was so spacious. It had four floors in total. The basement level was only accessible from the back of the house which meant that it was totally private. Adam was going to have a recording studio in there. He was really excited about it and couldn't wait for the work to start. It would be great for him to have that facility at home so that he could work whenever he wanted to. But it was the house itself that Clare really loved. She had spent the last few weeks overseeing the decorating and other minor works. It was all done now and she was absolutely delighted with the results. It really felt like theirs. She was happy just to wander from room to room, adjusting bits and bobs, changing things, moving ornaments, until she was satisfied then she would move on to the next room. She had decided that if she was ever in a position that she needed to look for alternative work she would like to be an interior designer. She had had so much fun with this house.

Adam came downstairs and they sat and drank their coffee together. The way things had worked out with the house had been ideal really. They came straight here from Nice – no need to go back to anywhere that held ghosts – this was a fresh start. They had spent their night in Nice talking until the small hours. Clare knew that Adam realised that he had made a stupid mistake and she accepted that they should move on and just put it behind them. She was convinced that it had been a one-off , a product of circumstance, and although she wasn't happy about it she knew that it hadn't meant anything to him. So she had put it to the back of her mind and hoped that it stayed there. With thoughts of baby Chloe still fresh in her mind she had brought up the subject of children. They were both in agreement that now that they were moving to a bigger house there was no reason to delay trying to start a family. The decision made, they had put the plan into action immediately.

Now, a few weeks on, Clare was beginning to suspect that she was actually pregnant. If that was the case the conception would definitely have taken place that night in Nice. Clare loved that idea. If she was pregnant she was going to be ecstatic anyway, but to think that their baby had been conceived in such a beautiful place was even better. But she didn't want to say anything to Adam yet. She didn't want to raise his hopes only to possibly have to dash them. So, for now, it was her secret. She spent ages looking at different pregnancy and baby websites. There were thousands. Sometimes she would get completely lost for hours, wading through the different sites. But she could do that here without Adam having any idea what she was looking at. In the flat he was invariably right by her side so there was no hiding what she was viewing. But here she had a lot more privacy if she needed it.

She looked across at Adam. He looked great. The few weeks off had done him good. He had the big charity gig coming up, which he was looking forward to, but it had been nice to have him at home all to herself for a few weeks whilst they had got settled into the house. The April sun, getting stronger by the day was streaming into the room. It was a large room on the ground floor. They had set it up as a formal dining room but by the French doors they had two chairs so that they could sit and admire the garden. As ever, Clare took great delight in ensuring that all the rooms were full of freshly cut flowers. This morning the room was heavy with the scent of lilies. She sat back contently, cradling her coffee. She realised that Adam was staring intently at her.

'Clare,' he began 'are you pregnant?'

Clare looked at him aghast. How could he know? She wasn't entirely sure herself yet!

'I don't actually know to be honest Adam' she said. 'I may be, but I haven't taken a test yet, I was waiting a bit longer. What makes you ask?' she was mystified.

He smiled. His eyes were shining as he leant forward and took her hands in his. 'You are. I can just tell,' he grinned 'you just have a look about you,' he rose from his chair and leaning towards her he tenderly wrapped his arms around her. 'Oh Clare. It will be *so* perfect. If you are pregnant now the baby will probably be here around about Christmas time. Can you imagine? Our first Christmas in our new house with a baby as well.' Clare snuggled closely into him. He was right. It would be difficult to imagine a more perfect scenario.

*

Blackpool Pleasure Beach didn't look particularly pleasurable to Janey. It looked decidedly tacky. In fact Blackpool itself wasn't looking too good. She had never been here before and had been looking forward to seeing the famous northern seaside town. The Las Vegas of the North it was sometimes called. Well, Janey had never actually been to Las Vegas either but she was thinking that it would probably be somewhat different to this. Maybe she was being uncharitable. It *was* early morning after all. She was sure it would look better at night when all the attractions were lit up. And of course it was the wrong time of year to see the main attraction – the illuminations which went the whole of the way down the promenade. But as Janey drove along it wasn't looking at it best. A few hardy souls were braving the wind and slight drizzle, wrapped up in warm coats and hats and scarves.

Janey pulled up at traffic lights and glanced across at what looked like a mum and her daughter. She wondered why they were out and about before anything was open. She looked again. It was Vara. She was sure of it. She was dressed very differently to the way Janey had been used to but there was no mistaking it, it was definitely Vara. And she had her daughter with her. What was her name? Daisy, wasn't it, yes, definitely Daisy Janey recalled. She sighed heavily. She hadn't really been in much doubt that Vara would have the audacity to come to this gig. She knew she would. But she wasn't looking forward to having to face her. She wondered what Vara's reasoning was behind bringing Daisy along. She had never brought her to a gig before. Was she hoping to hide behind Daisy, assuming that there would be no confrontations if the little one was there? Janey pondered. There would be no confrontation from her anyway. It wasn't her style. She was sad about what had happened but it was in the past now. She missed Vara's presence on the forum but things seemed to have settled down now and everything had more or less got back to normal. But this was Adam's first gig since the scandal and Janey had hoped that Vara might have had the decency to keep away at least for this one. But she had come to realise that conscience and sense of right from wrong weren't things that were high on Vara's priority list. What was best for Vara was what was important to her.

Janey drove on and found the car park which she had identified as being near to the venue. She parked up and walked over the road to the Winter Gardens. It wasn't just Adam performing at today's show. It was a charity gig and there were five big-name acts appearing with Adam being top of the bill and it was being shown live on TV. Janey was really looking forward to it. It was two months now since Union Chapel and she was desperate to see him again. It hadn't taken her long to forgive him for the Vara incident. He had sounded so heartbroken on the radio that day that her she had wept.

She didn't believe all the cynics who said that it had been a performance. She was convinced that it had been very genuine and her heart had gone out to him. She hoped that he and Clare had managed to get over it and were now happy again. She cared about him so deeply that his happiness was very important to her. She entered the Winter Gardens complex and followed the plan on the information board to find the Empress

Ballroom. As she approached she saw lines of people sitting on the floor. Indoor queuing, what a luxury – particularly in this weather. She saw Sarah and rushed up to her. It was always such a pleasure to see her friend again. She looked really well. The two women embraced, holding each other for a long time. A lot had happened in their world since the last time they had seen each other. Although they communicated regularly it was always good to see each other and enjoy that feeling that they only seemed to get between each other – the feeling of each one of them truly understanding the other. They finally let go of one another and Janey told Sarah that she had seen Vara and Daisy. Sarah rolled her eyes skyward. They had discussed the situation at length via the private message facility on OAFS and had both been convinced that Vara would be there. They would just have to see how it went. There was nothing they could do about it.

This gig was different. Instead of it just being Adam's fans lining up there were fans of all the other artists that were on the bill too. That was quite different and it added an extra dimension to the experience. They were also inside in the warmth for a change so it all added up to a bit of a party atmosphere. There were bars and cafes within the complex so they were relatively comfortable. Janey sat on the floor next to Sarah and they whiled away the hours chatting. Soon after Janey had arrived they had seen Vara and Daisy come in. Vara hadn't looked over at them and had chosen a place to sit which meant that she wasn't in their line of vision. It was easy to avoid her. Janey felt sad. She wanted things to be like they were before. The three of them had been such good friends. But Vara had put an end to that. There was no way that the gulf between them was ever going to be closed. Janey was certain of that. Metaphorically the small amount of physical space between them there in that hall in Blackpool was on an emotional level a million miles. It would never be crossed again.

Finally the doors opened to the ballroom. As the gig was being shown live on TV there had been stages set at either end of the ballroom. Apparently the plan was for the five acts to perform on alternate stages to allow for equipment changes without interrupting the continuous TV coverage. The trouble was, it was a guessing game as to which stage Adam was going to be on. If they made the right decision they would be at the front of the audience and if they made the wrong one, they would be at the back. Nightmare! All enquiries to the security staff had revealed nothing. They had to move fast. People were going both ways. They had to make a decision or else they wouldn't be right at the front of either stage. They went to the right. Having decided they ran and managed to get on the front row to the left of the stage. Janey turned to see where Vara was. She and Daisy had gone to the other stage. Janey hesitated. Did that mean that Vara knew something that they didn't know? She didn't trust her at all now and there she was, standing steadfastly in front of the other stage. Janey couldn't bear the thought that she and Sarah would have spent the whole day queuing only to find themselves at the wrong end. She looked at Sarah, they both looked back at Vara, but more and more people were streaming in now. Both ends were filling up. Even if they changed their minds now they wouldn't be on the front row. They stayed were they were.

They were right. As soon as the first act came on to their stage it was evident that the fifth act, Adam, would also be on that stage. They were ecstatic. They also had to admit to being delighted by the fact that Vara was at the wrong end. Childish, they knew, but it still gave them a smug sense of satisfaction.

The gig progressed, the other acts were great – it was good to see them, then Adam was on. No big build-up, no long wait, this was live TV and everything ran like clockwork. Janey felt the familiar surge of excitement as she looked at him, barely a meter away from her. That feeling never lessened in intensity. It was *so* good to see him again. He looked amazing. He wore tight black leather trousers and a plain white shirt; simple but very effective. He noticed them on the front row and he smiled at them. Janey felt herself melt. Those were the moments that she lived for. She might not be very good at trying to speak to Adam off stage but those moments when he made eye contact whilst he was singing were magical.

The gig finished and he was gone. It was early. The show had been scheduled for early evening TV and it was over much earlier than a normal gig. Knowing that this would be the case, Janey hadn't arranged to stay overnight. She could drive home, arriving in the early hours and then sleep in tomorrow as it was Sunday.

Anything to keep the costs down. She wasn't even going to hang about afterwards to see if Adam came out. It was a bit difficult to know where to go in this venue anyway. Where they had queued was indoors and there were many doors to the actual complex. It would be pure guess work to try and work out where Adam might exit the building. Given the circumstances Janey felt that he might just leave anyway, he wouldn't want to get involved in any tricky conversations with fans on this, his first public appearance since Union Chapel.

She said goodbye to Sarah and headed back to the car park. 10:00pm. If she got a good run home she could be in bed for 2:30. No rush to get up tomorrow. Happy and satisfied with the day she paid her car parking fee and walked back to her car. It was a multi-storey car park and Janey swiftly negotiated the ramps until she was at the bottom. She had to wait to pull out onto the road as a people carrier was just passing. She recognised it immediately. It was Adam's car. She would know it anywhere. She pulled out behind it and checked the number plate. Yep. Definitely, no question about it – that was Adam's car.

They stopped at traffic lights. Janey felt excited. She loved the thought that Adam was in that car even if she couldn't see him through the blacked out windows. She made her decision instantly. She would follow the car just to see where it was going. It was almost certainly going to go to a local hotel. She would just see where he was staying then she would continue on her way. A few more minutes weren't going to make any difference to her journey time.

She followed the car through the streets of Blackpool until they got to the outskirts of the town. He must be staying somewhere in the county Janey thought. She would need to be careful, she didn't want to end up pulling up the driveway of a country hotel closely behind the car. She would drop back a little bit so as not to make it too obvious. By now they were heading towards the motorway. Janey looked at a sign as they passed. This was the way she had come, they were heading back to London. Adam must be going straight home this evening too. Janey relaxed into her seat a little. Great, she would follow them all the way. That way she wouldn't need to concentrate on having to navigate as well as drive.

Just over four hours later they were on the outskirts of London. Adam's car had stopped briefly at a service station. Janey hadn't got out of her car as she didn't want to go in to use the bathroom and then miss them setting off again. So she sat in her car and watched as the four male occupants got out of the people carrier. No Clare. Janey wondered why not. She was usually there. There must be a reason why she hadn't been to the gig. Maybe that was why Adam was going straight home. She watched the four men walk across the car park towards the service building. Adam, Jason, Steve the bodyguard and the driver. After a while they re-emerged, all carrying take out coffee cups. They got back in the car and were off. Janey was right behind them.

Having followed the car all the way from Blackpool she might as well stay with it now, Janey reasoned. It would be nice to know where Adam lived after all. She wouldn't abuse the information but it would just be nice to know. They progressed through Hampstead and headed towards St John's Wood. They were still on the main route into central London when suddenly the car indicated right. Janey followed and they were soon driving down a residential road running parallel to the A41. Marlborough Hill. The houses were tall townhouses. Adam's car pulled up. He got out and said goodbye to the other occupants. He then crossed over the road and pulling a key out of his bag went into the house. As he closed the door the car pulled away. Janey took note of the house number then pulled away herself. Half an hour later she collapsed into bed. Exhausted but very, very happy.

*

Jason sank into bed. He was shattered, it had been a *really* long day. Steve had alerted them to the fact that they were being followed soon after they had left Blackpool. Sure enough, the small red Nissan had pulled into the services a discreet distance behind them and had then followed them out. Jason had tried to convince Adam not to go home, to come back with him to his flat. But he had been adamant. He had promised Clare that he would be home in the early hours and he wasn't going to be swayed. Using the advantage of the blacked out windows they had been able to identify the driver of the Nissan without her realising. They recognised her as one of the hardcore fans. Adam didn't recall ever really having spoken to her but he knew she was usually on the front row of the gigs. He had been convinced that she was harmless. She had probably just stumbled across their vehicle by chance, they were going the same way and she had decided to follow them on the spur of the moment.

Clare's pregnancy had been confirmed and Adam was determined that he wasn't going to let her down again. He had insisted, against Steve and Jason's advice that he was going home as planned. Jason had watched the Nissan pull up 50-meters down the road as Adam had crossed the road and let himself into his house. They had pulled off swiftly as soon as Steve was happy that Adam was safely inside the house. The driver then managed to tuck into an opening, out of sight. As the Nissan headed out of Marlborough Hill and rejoined the A-road heading into London they were able to reverse the tables and follow her. They stayed with her through the quiet city centre, their driver being much more adept at remaining undetected than she had been. Finally they watched as she pulled up outside a house in Streatham, South London and let herself in. Jason wrote down the address.

Jason tossed and turned. He wasn't as sure as Adam was that the fan was harmless. She had been alone so it wasn't a case of a few of them egging each other on. It had been a deliberate and calculated action. He had found it particularly disturbing that she had waited at the services. He really should have been more forceful with Adam about not letting him reveal his address. Adam was a huge star now. He had become much bigger than any of the other acts that Jason had managed previously, therefore he kept finding himself in unfamiliar territory, having to deal with situations that he hadn't come across before. For the last 3-years Adam had had a lot of ardent, devoted fans. Some of them seemed to follow him just about everywhere. But up until today Jason had never identified any behaviour that worried him.

A meeting with Adam was scheduled for Monday. Jason resolved that on Sunday he would do some research to see what he could learn about the psychological side of stalking. He wanted to be as informed as possible regarding some of the issues they may have to face in the future.

Feeling a little happier now that he had a plan of action he finally fell into a heavy sleep.

*

'Hi, Adam?' Vara had finally dialed Adam's number. She had established beyond doubt that she was pregnant a couple of weeks ago but she had held off from calling Adam. She had wanted to wait until after the Blackpool gig. She really hadn't known how it was going to go and she didn't want to complicate matters for herself by telling Adam prior to the gig. In the event Blackpool had been something of a disappointment for her. She had taken Daisy along. She knew that she would be ostracised by the OAFS so had felt that if she had Daisy with her she wouldn't feel so totally isolated. Anyway, it hadn't been an entirely selfish act, Daisy had been asking to go along to a gig for ages. This was a good one to take her to as it wasn't going to be such a late finish. It was also pretty local for them. She had driven the relatively short distance from Manchester to Blackpool.

Afterwards they had driven straight home again and Daisy was in bed well before midnight. But they had ended up being in front of the wrong stage. When the first act had come on and Vara had realised her mistake she had grabbed Daisy and they had made their way down the side. They got to within about five rows of the front but couldn't get any closer than that. Of course Daisy was far too short to be able to see anything from five rows back. Vara could see – but Adam couldn't see her. He wouldn't have even known she was there. Vara was bitterly disappointed. She had imagined him spotting her and smiling broadly. After all, she hadn't done anything wrong. It wasn't *her* that had sold the pictures to the papers. All she had done was confirm the story. Anyone in her position would have done the same. She was sure that if he had spotted her he would have been pleased to see her.

Adam gasped. He didn't usually take calls in the middle of meetings but he had seen that it was an unknown number and he was curious. He was fiercely protective over his phone number. Strangely, he recognised Vara's voice immediately. Considering the state that he had been in the last time they had spoken he wasn't entirely sure how he had managed to recognise her. But there was no doubt about it – this was Vara Reid. How on earth had *she* got his number?

'Yes' he replied to her query. 'This is Adam.' Gesturing to Jason that he would just be a minute he quickly let himself out into the garden. Jason was with him in the newly completed office/studio in the basement of his house. They were discussing Adam's upcoming Eastern European tour. Making sure that the door was securely closed he asked 'How did you get my number?'

Vara hadn't even told him who she was. She ignored his question. 'It's Vara' she said.

'I know. What do you want?' he hissed.

Vara remained calm. She had rehearsed this. 'I'm ringing to tell you that I am pregnant Adam,' she stated. The line went quiet. It remained quiet. 'Adam?' Vara wondered if he was still there – but the line hadn't gone dead, just quiet.

Adam sank down onto the garden seat that was fortunately right behind him. He cradled his head in his hands, still clinging on to the phone. He didn't know what to say or do. His head was spinning. He couldn't think straight. He couldn't seem to think at all.

'Adam?' Vara repeated.

Adam cut off the call. He remained where he was. Oblivious to Jason standing at the door looking at him he dropped his head. He needed space. This couldn't be happening. This situation had not even occurred to him. Not once. Not even in his darkest moments in Nice. Now he didn't know *why* he hadn't considered the possibility. The fact that he had no recollection of having had sex with this woman didn't alter the fact that he almost certainly had. Therefore, there was obviously the possibility that she could have become pregnant. Of course, he only had her word for that. If she was pregnant, and he assumed that she was, who's to say that he's the father? Adam shuddered. Even *thinking* of himself in that position made him feel ill. But either way – the thought of having to go down the road of paternity testing wasn't desirable either.

What on earth would he tell Clare? His eyes involuntarily went upwards to the house. Thank God she wasn't looking into the garden. She was probably taking a rest. She wasn't having an easy time of early pregnancy and she wasn't sleeping well.

Jesus Christ. What was he going to do? He needed to think fast. He had totally gone to pieces and he was just fortunate that Clare hadn't been there to witness it. Jason knew something was wrong but he was professional enough to know when to keep his distance. He and Adam had a close relationship but ultimately, Jason was employed by Adam.

Adam rang Vara back. 'What do you want from me?' he was curt.

She was prepared. 'What I want from you and what I am likely to get are two different things' she started. 'I would like you to be a responsible father to my – *our* child.' She thought she could just about hear him audibly shudder. 'However, I am a realistic person, I know that is unlikely to happen, therefore, I think it only reasonable that you contribute financially towards the cost of *your* child.' Again, he shuddered.

'How much?'

'£250,000.'

Adam sighed. The money wasn't the problem. If he honestly believed that he could give her £250,000 and never hear from or of her again he would send it around by courier now. But he didn't believe that would be the case for one minute. On the other hand he wasn't exactly in a position to draw up a legal proposal. He didn't want Clare to hear anything about this – ever.

'£250,000 – that's it and you never bother me again?' Even as he said it he doubted it.

'Yes' she declared. The line went quiet again. He needed time to think. Eventually he spoke again.

'I am going to end this call and I never want to hear from you again. I don't want to see you at the gigs, I don't want you to tell anybody who you *think* the father of your child may be. I will pass your number to a representative of mine who will contact you regarding payment. It will be a straightforward business transaction and you won't discuss any details with this person. *If* you stick to the terms of this agreement I will pay you the money in installments of £50,000 at 6-monthly intervals.'

It was Vara's turn to be quiet. Now *she* needed time to think. She hadn't expected him to completely give in immediately but she hadn't considered that *he* would impose conditions on *her*. It was supposed to be the other way around. She was rattled by the implication that he *wasn't* the father.

'Well?' he pressed.

'£100,000 every 6-months,' she countered.

He paused briefly.

'OK,' he conceded. 'But remember, if you ever try to

contact me personally again you won't get another penny.' He cut the line dead.

Adam remained in the garden for a few more minutes, regaining his composure. He didn't really believe that Vara would stick to her word but he hadn't really been in a position to argue. He would just have to live with it. He had got himself into this situation after all. It was no one's fault other than his own. Putting his phone back into his pocket he returned back to the studio with a smile.

'Coffee?' he asked Jason and proceeded to make the drinks as if their meeting had never been interrupted.

*

Red Square, Moscow. Sarah stood on the spot and slowly turned herself around, taking in her surroundings. She had travelled quite a lot in her life and seen many interesting places. But she had to admit, this one was one of the best. The wall surrounding the Kremlin to her left was quite simply the most impressive brick wall she had ever seen. It soared five meters upwards and seemed to stretch as far as the eye could see into the distance. At the end of the square stood St Basil's Cathedral which looked like something straight out of a fairytale. Today was hot. Hotter than hot. Moscow was experiencing its highest temperatures on record. The heat had come as something of a surprise to Sarah who had always had a mental imagine of Russia as being a cold, bitter place.

When the dates for Adam's Eastern European tour

had been announced Sarah had immediately been drawn towards the Russian gig. She had always fancied visiting Moscow and this seemed like the perfect opportunity. Dan wasn't enticed by the idea but her daughter, Jess, had leapt at the chance of joining her mum for a sojourn to Eastern parts. Jess was 20 and although not a massive Adam fan could usually be persuaded to join Sarah on trips to gigs in interesting places. But getting to Russia was no picnic. All visitors needed a visa, which wasn't easy to obtain then there were the difficulties of actually getting around in a country where English wasn't widely spoken.

However, they had managed it, they were here standing in the middle of Red Square being bowled over by the magnificence of the buildings before them. Sarah wasn't sure if it was the history and background of her surroundings or the presence of the smog and heat haze that made it all seem so very romantic to her. Either way, she was blown away. All the hassle and expense that she had gone through to get here had been worth it and they still had the concert to look forward to tonight.

They decided that they would walk around the perimeter of the Kremlin – all the way around the big red wall, a distance of almost a mile and a half. Despite the heat, they set off on their mission, determined to meet their goal. An hour later, just about ready to expire from the relentless midday sun they had made it back to the square. After making the latest of many purchases of bottled water they found a low wall to sit on and sat down to try and recover a little. The plan was that they would shortly make their way back to their hotel, shower, change, rest and then head out to the venue. They realised that there was no way on earth that they were going to be able to queue for very long in this heat so there was no point at all in rushing. Sarah closed her eyes as she started to feel the benefit of the ice cold water.

'Sarah.' Sarah opened her eyes quickly. But even through her sunglasses it was difficult for her eyes to adjust immediately. Who had spoken her name? It had been said confidently, there was no hint of a question – whoever it was clearly knew her well.

Sarah's eyes focused and she found herself staring straight at Vara. She was shocked. As far as Sarah knew, no other fans from the UK were coming to this gig. It was too complicated and expensive. It wasn't an easy option. But of course, those discussions had taken place on OAFS and Vara was no longer a part of the forum. Therefore, any plans that she made were unknown to everyone else.

Sarah took a moment to compose herself. Vara didn't jump in and say anything; no doubt anticipating that her presence would create a mixed reaction. In one respect Sarah was pleased to see another familiar place in these very unfamiliar surroundings. But her feelings towards Vara were still very mixed. She had no doubt that the money to fund Vara's trip would have come from her newspaper payment. Looking at her standing in front of her here it looked very much as though she was pregnant. Oh good grief. The possibility of Vara being pregnant with Adam's baby after their night together had certainly been a point of discussion between Sarah and Janey. They had just hoped that it wasn't the case. However, it looked as though it very much *was* the case. They knew that Vara didn't have a partner and from the look of her now, the timing would be right.

Sarah decided that she needed to talk to Vara. There was no point in ignoring her. Here they were both in a foreign country, clearing with plenty to talk about.

Finally, she broke her silence.

'Hello Vara, it's a surprise to see you here. You have met Jess before haven't you.' It wasn't a question, Jess had been at some of the same gigs as Vara. Vara smiled briefly at Jess.

'Shall we go somewhere for a coffee or a cold drink?' Sarah suggested. 'I think we have a lot of catching up to do.'

Vara said that her hotel was nearby and that they might as well go there. She led the way out of the square and the three women walked the short distance to the entrance of a very smart hotel overlooking the Bolshoi Theatre. Sarah sighed as she thought about the journey that she and Jess were going to have to take on the overheated underground train to get back to their modest hotel in the suburbs. Once again, she was in no doubt as to how Vara was funding this extravagance. She had no idea how much Vara would have been paid for spilling the beans about her and Adam but it wouldn't last forever if she was throwing it around like this. Vara had been used to surviving on a very tight budget and it looked like she had let her sudden change of fortune go to her head.

Sarah and Jess took a seat in the plush pleasantly cooled lounge area whilst Vara ordered the refreshments, finishing grandly with the command 'charge it to my room.' Against all her better instincts Sarah found it difficult not to smile. The last time she had spoken to Vara was way back in March on that fateful night outside Union Chapel in the wind and rain. Then, Vara had presented as a penniless, fairly desperate single mum. Now, a mere five months later she was swanning around in one of the best hotels in Moscow looking, and sounding, every bit the lady.

Unlike Janey, who would do anything to avoid confrontation, Sarah was a woman who wasn't afraid to speak her mind. She knew that Vara was also confident and at times outspoken so she saw no reason to hold back from coming straight to the point. As soon as Vara was settled in her seat Sarah spoke.

'So Vara. We miss you on OAFS, but I guess you chose your own path really. It was obvious that it would be pretty impossible to return to the forum after what you had done.' She paused briefly but never broke eye contact with Vara. 'How do you feel now? Any regrets?'

Vara held Sarah's gaze.

'Not one,' she replied boldly. 'I don't think that I did anything that anyone else in my position wouldn't have done. Nothing about that night was planned or preconceived.'

Sarah baulked slightly at Vara's blatant choice of word and glanced at Jess who raised her eyes skywards.

'It certainly wasn't me that went to the papers with those pictures. If it had been up to me the whole thing would have begun and ended that night,' she continued. She then glanced down at her rounded belly which protruded slightly underneath her expensive looking summer top. 'Well, apart from this of course' she added, gently patting her bump.

Sarah sighed. *If* there had been no pictures, *if* Vara had managed to keep her mouth shut about the whole thing initially- the story would have broken eventually when the pregnancy became apparent. Vara wasn't the sort of girl that was going to sit on a potential goldmine in terms of paparazzi payments.

'So what's the deal now?' Sarah asked. 'Are you going to go to the papers again with the pregnancy?'

Vara lifted her glass to take a drink. She wasn't going to answer that immediately. She would let Sarah and Jess think about it for a few moments. It had certainly crossed her mind. But she had concluded that she was probably onto a better thing getting money from Adam. For a start, she liked the idea of having Adam's money much better than receiving anonymous payments from the media. She was astute enough to realise that she couldn't have both. She couldn't blackmail Adam *and* sell her story. She had no intention of letting Adam get away with the five payments that she had originally agreed to. He was rich enough after all so she saw no reason why he couldn't continue to make regular payments for as long as he needed to keep her quiet. Which would be forever. He had fallen into *that* trap himself. She knew how important it was to him that Clare didn't find out about her pregnancy. In believing he was buying her continuing silence by spreading the payments out he had created a scenario that was going to be impossible for him to break. She would just continue to repeat her demands. That way she was guaranteed a life of luxury, hence her extravagant trip to Russia. She had it made. She placed her glass down on the table and looked directly at Sarah.

'No' she stated indignantly. 'I won't be going to the papers. This is a private matter between Adam and me'.

Sarah was just taking a sip of her own drink. She spluttered, almost choking. She could barely believe what she was hearing. She had always known that Vara wasn't lacking in self-confidence. But to have the audacity to imply that she had some sort of ongoing relationship with Adam was almost beyond belief. It was evident to Sarah that Adam and Clare were still very much together and indeed, it had recently been confirmed that Clare was pregnant. Sarah was still trying to get her head around the whole complicated situation. She couldn't believe for one minute that Vara was part of some cosy little arrangement with Adam. She really didn't know what she *did* believe at this stage but whatever the truth was she was sure there would be money in it for Vara somewhere along the line. Finishing her drink she looked at Jess and indicated that she was ready to make a move.

'Well Vara. It isn't an easy situation that you are in. I am sure that you want what is best for your baby. But as Adam is clearly in a happy and stable relationship I do hope that you manage to respect that.' She stood up. 'And now, I think that it is time that Jess and I were getting back to our hotel. Thank you for the drinks. We will no doubt see you later'. With that she and Jess strode back across the busy lounge and out of the hotel. Sarah's head was in a spin. She couldn't even begin to believe that Vara would have considered leaving Adam alone and not involving him in some way in her pregnancy. She knew that wouldn't be the case. But how on earth was it going to work? Both Clare and Vara were pregnant with Adam's babies. Despite the stifling heat which hit them once more as soon as they walked through the hotel door, Sarah shivered.

*

Adam stood rooted to the spot. He had been standing looking idly out of his hotel room window when he had seen them. Three of his fans walking across the road in front of the hotel and one of them was Vara Reid. He watched them until they were out of sight. They hadn't entered this hotel. He supposed he should be thankful at least for that. But she was here. That was bad enough. He slumped down into a chair as all of his worst nightmares came back to haunt him. He had played over so many different scenarios in his mind since the dreadful day that she had phoned him. He imagined her coming face to face with Clare – both visibly pregnant. On really bad days he had pictured the same scene but with him standing in between them – with Clare looking questioningly at him. He really didn't know how he would cope with such a situation. No matter how many times he had been over it in his head, so as to be prepared just in case it did happen, it never got any easier and he never got any nearer to finding an acceptable solution. Because there wasn't one.

If Clare ever discovered that Vara Reid was pregnant with his child that would be the end of their relationship. He had absolutely no doubt about that. He really couldn't bear the thought of that happening. The few days that he had spent in Nice when they had been apart from each other had been complete torture. But the situation that he was in now was also torturous. He hated himself for being deceitful. He had never had any secrets before, never held anything back from Clare. She knew everything about him. Until now. In the last few months he had had to try and accept that this was something that he was just going to have to learn to live with. There was to be no happy ending, no magical solution.

Staring blankly out of the window he sighed heavily. He had been astonished at the splendour and majesty of Moscow. He was overwhelmed by the magnificence and grandeur that surrounded him. Now he just felt hollow. Clare wasn't with him. She really wasn't having an easy time of pregnancy and she didn't want to take any chances as far as the baby was concerned. They knew that Eastern Europe was in the middle of a heat wave and so reluctantly they had agreed that she would stay at home whilst Adam completed the short tour. There would be other times, they said. That was the plan anyway. Plenty more opportunities for them to travel together at some future date. Adam closed his eyes and sighed again. Sometimes he daren't even *think* about the future. When he was with Clare he happily went along with all her plans as she mapped out where they might be and what they might be doing this time next year, in 5 years, in 10 years. She loved those sort of conversations, building up a cosy picture of the three of them as a happy little family. Adam loved it too. He wanted it to be like that more than he wanted anything. But the dull, sickening feeling at the bottom of his stomach was never far away. It was like a heavy black cloud hanging over his head, threatening to burst at any moment.

Why is she here? He told her to keep away from the gigs. Why wasn't she sticking to her part of the bargain? It wasn't fair. He frowned to himself, realising how stupid he was being. Whoever said that blackmail was fair? Of course it wasn't fair. There was nothing even remotely fair about it. He was being held to ransom. His favourite pastime was the one where he allowed himself to imagine that he could turn back the clock. That he could somehow erase that night in the Kings Cross hotel. And his worse moments were when reality hit him again and he knew that no matter how much he wanted it and wished for it, it was never going to happen.

*

The Arena Club Moscow was a new venue, just opened that year. It was a fantastic place, having the feel of a club but with the proportions of a small arena. Adam had never played in a place like this and normally he would have been very excited. This was his first performance in Russia and the crowd were going wild. He stood in the wings, peeping carefully around the edge of the curtain. Before he was even on stage he knew that Vara was there, on the front row. Not right in the centre thankfully, but just to the right. But at least now that he knew where she was he would be able to avoid her. The last thing he wanted when he was in the middle of singing a heartfelt line would be to catch her eye. He clearly hadn't been able to stop her attending gigs but he could certainly try and avoid looking at her.

Jason watched Adam looking around the curtain. He knew something was wrong but he didn't know what. Sometimes these days Adam could be very secretive. Jason was concerned. It wasn't like Adam. It all seemed to stem from the day that their meeting in Adam's studio had been interrupted by a phone call. And that was immediately after the incident where the fan had followed Adam home from Blackpool. Jason wondered if the two events were linked. He didn't have a clue *how* the fan could have got Adam's phone number, but maybe she had. Maybe it was her that had called him that morning and Adam would have been reluctant to tell Jason. If she was a serious stalker then he, Jason would have been right and Adam should have listened to him that night and not gone straight home. But surely if Adam was being harassed by a stalker he would confide in Jason?

Adam took his cue and bounded onto the stage. The crowd went berserk. Watching from the side, Jason relaxed. Everything was fine. Adam was his usual polished self, playing to the audience, working them to his advantage. It really was a joy to watch him perform and to see how each audience responded. Jason had worked in Russia before and he knew that the local crowds were generally very lively. Then suddenly Jason heard Adam's voice falter as he sang a particularly long note. That *never* happened. He looked more closely. There was a commotion going on at the front of the audience. The heat in the building was almost unbearable and for the people squashed in at the front it must have been particularly bad. Someone must have fainted. Jason watched as a young woman was manhandled over the barrier. A security guard carried her to the wings. She was clearly pregnant. Jason was concerned for the woman's welfare and rushed forward to ensure that she received the relevant care. As he approached her and looked at her face he felt a shock wave run through him. He recognised her immediately. It was Vara Reid.

*

The bright red, gleaming Ferrari sat proudly on the drive. Well, to be honest, it couldn't strictly speaking be described as a drive. It was a parking space at the front of the house. At some point in the building's history a previous owner had converted the front garden into this useful facility.

Clare sat at the kitchen table looking out. She liked the rather unusual layout of the house which meant that the spacious kitchen was at the front. She spent many an hour sitting here watching the world go by and day dreaming. She wasn't finding pregnancy easy. She had expected to sail through it just as her sister, Helen, had done. But it hadn't been the case for Clare. Now, almost six months down the line, she was hoping that the final trimester was going to be a bit easier. She was very thankful that she was in a position where she was able to choose whether to work or not. If she felt up to it she would get in touch with Adam's team and see what needed to be done. But she didn't have to. There were plenty of people that were very capable of keeping things afloat. It was quite nice in a way just to be able to take things a bit easier and take more of a back seat.

They had both worked so very hard over the last few years, she felt that now they were reaping the benefits. They loved their new home and the Ferrari, Adam's first real extravagance, had been delivered a couple of weeks ago. Adam wasn't normally one for such lavishness but this had always been his one big dream. Clare smiled as she remembered his excitement on the day that it had arrived. If he had grinned any wider his face would have split! He was over the moon with it. With his encouragement Clare had taken a little drive in it herself, with him at her side of course. But quite frankly, she was frightened of it. She felt as though it had a wild animal hiding in the engine ready to pounce as soon as she touched the accelerator. But she loved being the passenger when Adam was driving, especially out in the countryside. They had started to think about getting a second home. So before Adam had headed off to Eastern Europe they had taken a couple of drives out of London. They had loved cruising around the country roads and stopping off at quiet pubs for lunch. Nearly always Adam would be recognised but he always dealt with it politely and calmly and it wasn't really a problem. It just went with the job. Clare would wait patiently in the background whilst he posed for photos or signed autographs.

Adam was due home today. Clare couldn't wait. He had only been away for just over a week and they had talked several times a day but it had still seemed like forever. She had been busy whilst he was away though. She had been shopping with Helen and Chloe and bought lots of baby equipment and clothes. Clare loved spending time with them and Helen was able to offer invaluable advice on what was worth buying and what wasn't. It also gave Clare the opportunity to spoil Chloe rotten too which she loved doing.

She couldn't wait for Adam to get home and see how the nursery had filled up in the last week. It was just about ready now, everything in place. All they had to do now was try and be patient as they waited for the baby to arrive. That would be the hard part. Although Clare knew that she still had a long way to go, she was so desperate for the baby to be born that she just wanted it to happen now. Clare checked the time on the kitchen clock. Noon. Adam's driver was coming at 1:00pm to take her to Heathrow in the Ferrari to meet Adam. Not long now. She could hardly contain her excitement. He would be able to tell her all about his trip as they drove home.

She saw him the moment the arrivals door slid open. She had the advantage of course as she was focusing exclusively on a very small defined area. Adam had to scan through all the crowds of people standing waiting for arriving passengers. Clare rushed forward and threw herself straight into his arms. The embrace went on and on. Clare buried her face into his shoulder and he held her close. Neither of them wanted to let go. Finally Adam eased his grip on her and held her at arm's length. She looked great. Her week with Helen and Chloe buying London out of baby goods had obviously done her the world of good. She beamed widely at him, she was *so* delighted to see him. He hoped that the turmoil that was running through him wasn't showing. Since the Moscow gig his emotions had been all over the place. Trying to concentrate on his performance as he saw an obviously pregnant Vara Reid being pulled over the barrier in full view of all of his band, crew and Jason had been almost impossible. He knew that they were all aware who she was. She had always been a very visible fan both during and after the gigs. Then of course there had been the pictures in the papers, both the initial ones and the follow up article. He was in no doubt that as she was carried away in front of the stage everybody would have seen her and drawn their own conclusions. Nobody had said anything to him, not even Jason but he knew that they knew. He was in complete turmoil now. What on earth was he going to do? There was no point in continuing to pay her money if she was going to blatantly disregard his requests. But the possible, no, probable consequences if he didn't pay her didn't bear thinking about. It was already bad enough. But so far Clare didn't know.

He pulled her close to him again. He wanted to wrap her in cotton wool and protect her from what he had begun to accept was the inevitable. Instead he put his arm around her and they walked to the Ferrari. Taking a deep breath he smiled and tried to concentrate on her tales of what she had been doing and how fantastic the nursery looked now. But his head was still in Moscow and the images he saw were not of Red Square and the Kremlin.

*

Janey sat in her car half-way down Marlborough Hill. She knew that she shouldn't be here. But it was a Sunday – she had nothing else to do. It was 3-months since she had last seen Adam and she was desperate to have a sighting of him, even just a quick glimpse would be enough. It wasn't as if she was a stalker or anything. She was just a fan. She just wanted to see him. There was no way that she would have been able to go any of the Eastern European concerts. She didn't have the money or enough holidays. So therefore she told herself, it was perfectly acceptable behaviour to be sitting just down the road waiting for Adam to arrive home from his trip.

It wasn't as if she was going to bother him or invade his privacy. She was only going to look at him. She had heard via Sarah that Clare hadn't been with him in Moscow so she had probably gone to the airport to pick him up. She had also heard from Sarah the news regarding Vara. Janey was deeply upset to learn that Vara was pregnant. That had been her worst fear. She knew that Vara would be incapable of keeping it a secret and it worried Janey as to how it was going to affect Clare. Whatever happened it was bound to have a negative effect on Clare and Adam's relationship. Adam's happiness mattered more than anything to Janey. She cared about him so much that she hated the thought of him being miserable.

As she sat pondering, the Ferrari pulled into the road and the grace and elegance of the vehicle took Janey's breath away. She watched as Adam pulled across the road then expertly reversed it into the parking place in front of his house. She slunk down in her seat so as not to be seen as Clare and Adam opened the doors and got out of the car. Smiling and chatting to each other they walked the short distance to the front door. Just as Clare was unlocking the door Janey saw another car pull up. Steve, the bodyguard got out and unloaded Adams luggage. Together they carried the bags into the house. Adam closed the front door and Steve pulled away. Janey sank further down into her seat as Steve's car passed. She thought she detected the other car slowing down as it passed but no, she must have been imagining it. She was getting paranoid. Why would he slow down as he passed her car? He would have no idea who she was or why her car was there. Don't worry about it she told herself. And she didn't. Within seconds the incident was out of her mind and she was once again concentrating on Adam's house.

She would just stay a bit longer. She knew that realistically there was little chance of her seeing Adam again today. He was just back from a trip away and he and Clare had just been reunited. But somehow she didn't seem to be able to drive away. She would stay a little bit longer. It gave her a warm feeling to know that Adam was close by.

Lost in her dream world she was totally unaware that Steve was parked just a few cars away from her, watching her very closely in his rear view mirror. He stayed there until finally three hours later she left.

*

Daisy ran from room to room in the empty flat. She was *so* excited. Mum said that this was going to their new house. Imagine that! Living in this big tall building. It even had a lift that worked. Some of her friends lived in tall blocks of flats but they weren't smart like this one and the lifts were usually broken. This flat was very smart and it even had a little garden on the roof which would just be for them! It had a lovely big bedroom for her, a bedroom for mum and another one for the new baby. Mum's bedroom even had its own bathroom! That meant that she and the baby would have a bathroom all to themselves. She did a little dance in the middle of the vast empty living room. It had patio doors leading onto a little balcony and she was sure that she could see the whole of Manchester from here. Mum said that at night time the lights would be beautiful. She just couldn't wait. But she had to. The baby was due just before Christmas and mum said that they would be moving in sometime just before that. Maybe it would be November thought Daisy. That would be good because they would then be able to put up their advent things almost as soon as they moved in. Daisy had a special advent tree with 24 little boxes and each day there was a small surprise in each box. She wondered on which of the days the baby would be born. It was *really* special to be expecting a baby brother or sister so close to Christmas. Next year the baby would have to have an advent tree too. She did another little dance as a lovely warm feeling engulfed her. She was *so* happy.

Vara stood on the balcony surveying the view before her. The estate agent hadn't lied. This really was an incredible outlook. She turned back and looked into the flat. Daisy was rushing from room to room and appeared to periodically be performing some sort of mad rain dance. Vara smiled. It was lovely to see her daughter looking so happy. It would be fantastic for them to be able to live here in this beautiful, spacious apartment after being so cramped up on the ground floor of a terraced house. Vara had it all worked out. Years of living on virtually no money meant that she knew how to do her sums. Ok, so the figures that she was dealing in now were considerably larger than the ones she had previously being used to but the principles were the same. It was all about budgeting. Her second payment from Adam was due next week. She would put all of that down as a deposit. She still had money left over from her first payment so she was ok for living expenses. Having paid her deposit she would then be able to move into the flat. For the six months until her next payment was due from Adam she would pay a mortgage. Then, when the next payment came she would pay off her mortgage and that would be that. The flat would be hers. Perfect. Nothing could go wrong. She had had to be a little inventive when it came to proving where her funding was coming from though. The money laundering regulations meant that she had to be very specific as to how she had got the money. It wasn't sufficient apparently to just turn up with money and say you wanted to buy a property. The authorities had to be satisfied that you hadn't procured your funds from illicit activities such as drug dealing etc. Initially this had all come as a shock to Vara. Never before having been in the position to even think about buying her own property, she had no idea that such regulations were in place. However, necessity being the mother of invention, she had worked her way around it. The skills that she had honed when she needed to evade paying her fare on the trains or paying her Visa bills came in to play once more. Good heavens she thought to herself when she realised that that had only been earlier this year. Standing here in her designer clothes, about to put a deposit down on a penthouse flat, she could hardly comprehend that fact. But it was true.

She had proof that money already in her current account had come from a newspaper payment. That wasn't a problem. As to the money paid from Adam, she had quite simply stated that it was maintenance payments. She couldn't see a problem with that. She had considered going down the line of pretending that she was a backing singer or something. But on thinking about it she realised that backing singers don't get paid *that* much money. So she decided to just tell the truth. After all, that's what they were. Maybe some people would see it as blackmail but she really didn't see why Adam shouldn't be expected to pay towards the upkeep of his own child. Her conscience was perfectly clear.

'Come on Daisy. Time to go. It won't be long now until we can come back and start to move our things in'. Vara gave her delighted daughter a little squeeze as she bundled her out of the door. 'Let's go home and start packing'.

*

Today a photographer was coming to take pictures of the house. Clare was fussing around ensuring that everything was just so. When she had been approached by the glossy magazine about them doing a feature on her home she had jumped at the chance. She hated cheap nasty paparazzi coverage of anything to do with Adam and herself but the chance for her home to be featured in an up-market quality publication was something that really appealed to her. She had thoroughly enjoyed the process of transforming this house into what she wanted and especially now that the nursery was ready she relished the chance to show it off. Maybe people would be impressed and she may get commissioned to do some interior design for others. She would enjoy that. The journalist had already written up the article, it was just the pictures that needed taking now. Hopefully the piece would be in the November issue.

Adam hadn't been too impressed with the idea. She had told him about it when he had returned from his Eastern European tour and she had expected him to be happy for her. He knew that the house was important to her and how much she had enjoyed the project. She thought that like her, he would be happy to see something positive in print about them. But his attitude had seemed to be that he didn't want any type of exposure regarding his private life. She had been a little put out but had gone ahead with it anyway. She was happy generally to be in the background but felt strongly that if there was something that she really wanted to do then she should go ahead and do it. She did still have her own life after all.

The photographer went from top to toe of the house taking pictures from all angles of every room. Adam drew the line at pictures being taken of his studio though. That was his own private space and he wasn't having pictures of that being spread all over the place. That wasn't a problem as far as Clare was concerned though. She had had nothing to do with the plans for the studio and it could hardly be classed as interior design.

Having satisfied himself that he had enough shots of the empty rooms the photographer then wanted to take some pictures of Adam and Clare relaxing in their home. Once again, Clare noticed Adam's reluctance. She really couldn't see a problem with them being portrayed as a happy expectant couple eagerly awaiting the birth of their first child. That was what they were after all. But Adam seemed to have a problem with it. His attitude was beginning to upset her and she was almost on the verge of tears. Noticing this Adam relented and agreed to have pictures taken in the nursery and living room. With harmony once again restored the photographer finished the shoot and left. After she had let him out of the front door Clare went to find Adam. She was keen to talk to him to see if she could establish why he had been so reluctant to participate in the photo session. But he had already gone done to the studio. She really didn't want to negotiate the outdoor steps that led down from the dining room. They were covered in autumn leaves and her increasing size didn't make it easy.

Clare went into the kitchen and put the kettle on. She would just leave him. He would be back up later and maybe he would be a bit more relaxed after a session in the studio. She couldn't imagine that there was an underlying agenda to his grumpiness. He would be fine. She would just give him time to get over it. With that she made her coffee, sat down at the kitchen table and allowed her thoughts to return to soft furnishings. She couldn't wait to see the finished magazine article.

*

The spreadsheet was confusing Sarah. She was organising an OAFS Christmas party. It had seemed like a good idea to begin with but it was all getting a lot more complicated than she had anticipated. Adam was doing a gig at the O2 in London in early December. It was a Friday night. A lot of people would be travelling so they had decided that it would be a good idea to make a weekend of it. They would have a great time at the gig on the Friday, spend Saturday however they wanted, sightseeing or Christmas shopping then on Saturday night they could have a party. On Sunday, when they had all recovered from their hangovers they could make their way home. Perfect.

Well, that was the theory anyway. But when Sarah had looked into making a booking for a restaurant it had all begun to get more complicated. Firstly they all had to agree on where to go. Should they go for a party boat? What about booking a private room? What about the people who couldn't really afford very much? The discussions went on for weeks. When they finally agreed on a place great debates began again regarding the menu. Should they just go for the ordinary menu or opt for the set Christmas menu? Sarah was beginning to wish she had never suggested a party in the first place.

Eventually it had been decided that they would go for the set Christmas menu and the booking had been made. That is when it started to get even more complicated. A deposit had to be paid and then the balance would need to be settled 4-weeks before the event. On top of that, everyone had to state what they wanted to eat from the menu choices. Sarah looked again at the spreadsheet. She had a list of names, whether they had paid a deposit or the full amount, what they wanted for starter, main and dessert. She had lists of people who had paid her online, people who were to pay her on the night – she also had a mental list of one or two who she doubted would *ever* pay her. However, as much as it had proved to be more of a headache than she had imagined, the prospect of the party, well, the whole weekend was fun. She could hardly wait. She hadn't seen any of the OAFS for ages and all her friends were planning on being there. It would be a great atmosphere particularly as it was December. The timing was perfect. She was also desperate to see Adam again.

It seemed like forever since that hot night back in August in Moscow. Looking out of the window now at the dank dreary weather it almost seemed like another world. She wondered what had become of Vara. She had been concerned when she had fainted at the gig but she hadn't been surprised. That was no environment for a pregnant woman to be in. It was way too hot and she must have been extremely squashed up against the barrier. She certainly didn't seem to have been thinking of her baby's welfare. Sarah also wondered about the effect that the scene had had on Adam. She had seen him looking and sensed that it had knocked him off his stride momentarily but he had recovered his composure quickly.

After the gig, much to the locals' disappointment, he had driven straight away without doing any signings. This was extremely unusual and Sarah could only assume that he had been unnerved by what he had witnessed. She had discovered that Clare hadn't accompanied him on the tour but surely, if she didn't already know about Vara's pregnancy it was only a matter of time before she did. Sarah couldn't begin to imagine the kind of devastating effect that it would have on Adam and Clare's relationship. She really felt for them as she honestly did believe that it had all been just a silly mistake on Adam's part (aided and abetted in no small way by Vara). The consequences of this mistake however were set to be potentially catastrophic as she didn't believe for one minute that Vara would keep the story out of the papers forever. Although she honestly did have sympathy for Adam and Clare she also had to admit that she was worried on a personal level. A major upset in Adams private life was bound to have consequences and repercussions on his public image. They had already begun to see changes, like him not meeting the fans after gigs. What would happen if he and Clare split up and it affected him so badly that he didn't perform anymore? Sarah knew that she was being melodramatic but she really *was* concerned. She didn't like to think of him as being upset but she hated even more the thought that she wouldn't be able to see him perform. It didn't bear thinking about.

Sarah was also beginning to get a little worried about Janey. After Sarah's return from Moscow Janey had let it slip that she had been sitting in Adam's street. She had tried to wrap it up to make it all sound very innocent, as if she had just kind of been passing and realised that Adam was probably about due home from the airport. Sarah's knowledge of London wasn't brilliant but she knew enough to know that it would be highly unlikely that Janey would have just been passing Adam's house. From that point on Sarah had been ultra-sensitive to whatever Janey posted or said. She seemed to be picking up hints and clues all over the place that Janey was turning into a fully fledged stalker. She sighed to herself as she remembered those early days when Adam was new on the scene, The Adam Olsen Fan Club was in its infancy and everybody was happy and excited. Oh, to be able to go back to those days! But life was life and nothing ever stood still. She would just plod on organising the party, looking forward to the gig and hoping against hope that everything would work out ok.

On the forum there was a little smiley face that wore rose-tinted glasses. Somehow Sarah got the feeling that she could do with them right now.

*

Adam had made the decision to stop making payments to Vara Reid shortly after his return from Russia. He had been absolutely outraged at what she had done, blatantly flouting the terms of their agreement. There was no way that he was going to continue giving her money. The secret so-called was going to be out anyway. If she had the audacity to attend gigs and parade herself on the front row she obviously had no intention of showing him any respect by trying to keep her pregnancy secret. Adam just had to face the fact that Clare was going to find out sooner or later. He just wished that he had the guts to tell her to her face. That would be so much more courageous of him. But he just had to cling on to the last vestiges of hope that somehow she might not find out. He knew that it was a vain hope really, it was much more likely that pigs would fly, but whilst there was still a glimmer of hope, no matter how small, he wanted to cling on to it. She was so happy in her little bubble, he couldn't bear the thought of bursting it.

Today he was heading into town in a cab to meet with Jason and Steve. They wanted to discuss another troublesome fan; the female who followed them back from Blackpool. Adam was still sure that she was totally harmless but Jason and Steve seemed convinced otherwise. They wanted to take action so Adam had agreed to meet them to discuss the situation. Looking out of the window at the overcast London skyline he sighed. Life had become so very complicated lately.

Steve had come to the meeting prepared. He had documental and photographic evidence that Janey Richmond, a woman in her forties from South London was stalking Adam. She had been seen on no less than ten occasions sitting in her car, a small red Nissan, in Marlborough Hill. She had also been observed following Adam and Clare on shopping expeditions. Adam was shocked. He had had no idea that this had been going on. Why was she doing this? What could she hope to gain from it? She had never approached him (thank goodness) but he would have been able to understand it more easily if she had. If she had wanted to talk to him. But just to follow him, that was creepy.

Jason had also been doing his homework. He reported that stalkers generally fall into one of two categories: psychotic and non-psychotic. Most stalkers apparently fall into the non-psychotic category meaning that they have no pre-existing psychotic disorders. As much as Adam appreciated the fact that Steve and Jason were doing their jobs and trying to protect him he couldn't really see why it mattered which sort of stalker this woman was. A stalker was a stalker – and he didn't want one.

'What can we do about it?' he asked.

'As we have plenty of evidence we can apply for a restraining order under the Protection from Harassment Act,' Steve replied. This will prevent her from lawfully coming anywhere near you or your home.

'Let's do it,' replied Adam and stood up to leave.

Outside Adam went to buy Clare some flowers before hailing a cab to take him home. He had turned down Jason's request that he use the regular car and driver for his journey today. Sometimes he liked to just try and hang on to a little bit of independence and not have everything done for him. It could get so stifling. However, the meeting had unnerved him. Maybe he should have used the car and driver after all. Looking over his shoulder as he left the florists he climbed into the cab resolving that from now on he would do as Jason suggested. Somehow he suspected that certainly at the moment Jason was a little more capable of logical, sensible thinking than he was.

*

Vara threw her phone down onto the sofa. She had spent the last 40-minutes speaking to the bank. She had been passed through numerous automated systems before she had finally been able to speak to a live person. It was ridiculous. And even then she hadn't had any joy. Adams payment was a week overdue now. She had left it a couple of days before she had started to make enquiries as sometimes things do get delayed. However, this was the fifth day now that she had spoken to someone and it was still the same answer. 'Sorry Ms Reid. No new payments.'

Vara was furious. That was it, she wasn't waiting any longer. Retrieving her phone from its resting place on a cushion she dialed Adam's number. No reply. Over the next hour she dialed Adam's number continuously. With every failed attempt she was getting increasingly enraged. How could he do this to her? Didn't he have any sense of responsibility? He had entered into an agreement with her. Ok, she had gone to a gig, but she hadn't gone anywhere near him. She had had no intention of queuing up to see him after the gig even if she hadn't been incapacitated. She hadn't wanted to jeopardise her payments. It wasn't her fault that she had ended up being dragged over the barrier. This was just all so unfair.

She eventually slammed the phone down onto the sofa again in pure frustration. She was late with her deposit for the flat. If she didn't have the money by the end of the week she would lose the flat. And she *so* wanted it. She went to make herself a coffee in the pokey little kitchen. She looked around her in disgust. Mentally she had already moved out of here. For weeks now she had been picturing herself gliding around her new spacious ultra modern apartment. She had imagined herself and Daisy sitting at the beautiful sleek table that she had ordered, whilst the baby snoozed peacefully in the Moses basket. Now all her dreams appeared to be collapsing around her. Well, she wasn't having it. She wasn't going to let Adam get away with it. She wasn't going to stay here, slipping back into living in poverty whilst he lived in his fancy house in London with his cosy little family. Reaching for her phone again she dialed a number. Unlike the bank, it was answered in seconds

'News desk please.' Settling down onto the sofa she prepared to rock Adam Olsen's cosy little world to its foundations.

*

Hundreds of magazines faced Janey as she quickly scanned the supermarket shelf. She didn't buy them very often so she wasn't familiar with the shelving system and where she needed to be looking. Eventually, just as she was thinking that she may need to seek assistance to find what she was looking for she saw it: the glossy homes magazine that had the article about Adam and Clare in it. There had been a huge amount of discussion on OAFS about it and she had been desperate to get a copy as soon as it was published. As she pulled it out from its position half tucked behind another magazine she gasped. She hadn't realised that they were going to be featured on the front cover. The picture was beautiful. It showed the couple standing next to an empty ornate antique crib. Clare's hands were resting on the side of the cradle and Adam was behind her, his arms wrapped protectively around her protruding stomach. The photographer had done a fantastic job. The picture spoke volumes. They looked like the happiest couple that had ever lived. The air of expectancy exuded from the image. The magazine was wrapped in a plastic cover so Janey was unable to look inside. She decided that it didn't matter about getting any other shopping, she would just quickly pay for the magazine then she could go and sit in her car and read the article.

Settling into the driver's seat a few minutes later she pulled open the packaging and quickly found the feature. There were several more pictures as well as quite a lengthy interview. Janey read it quickly then read it again, more slowly this time, allowing the words to penetrate. The interview was with Clare, not Adam. She explained in depth about how she had chosen the colour scheme for each room, where they had come by all the different antiques, fixtures and fittings etc. Janey found the article interesting, but it was the pictures that really transfixed her, even the ones which just showed empty rooms. To Janey it was fantastic to have this insight into Adam's home. She found herself imagining him walking between the different rooms, sitting in this chair, lying in that bed.

Eventually Janey realised that she had been sitting in her car in the supermarket car park for rather a long time and she was cold. She had better go home. She positioned the magazine carefully on the seat beside her so that she was able to glance at the cover every time that she needed to stop. As she drove, her thoughts turned to the 02 gig. It wouldn't be long now, she couldn't wait. She hadn't seen the OAFS for ages and she was so desperate to see Adam again. She had got into a bit of a habit of driving down his street on a weekend but it wasn't like *really* seeing him. A lot of the times that she went to Marlborough Hill she didn't even see him anyway. Sometimes she would sit there for ages and maybe all that she would see would be a light being turned on in a room. Occasionally she saw Adam and/or Clare coming or going but not very often. She had on the odd occasion followed them on their outings. Not with any malicious intent obviously, just because she had nothing else to do and she just *liked* watching Adam. But as much as that gave her a taste she really needed more. She was counting the days to the gig. She pulled into her road and found a parking space. Picking up the precious magazine she got out of her car and headed to her front door. She let herself in and was just closing the door behind her when she realised that someone was about to knock.

'Janey Richmond?' the smartly dressed middle aged man asked.

'Yes' she answered, curious as to who he was and how he knew her name.

Handing her an envelope he proffered his record of delivery notice which she signed. Intrigued, she closed the door pulling open the official looking envelope as she made her way to the kitchen. She threw her bag and the magazine onto the table as she quickly scanned the letter. The blood drained from her face as she stared at the document. It was an injunction preventing her from going anywhere near Adam or his home. It prohibited her from attending any of Adam's public performances. Her eyes began to sting as tears filled them. She felt her legs beginning to weaken beneath her and instinctively she felt behind her for a seat which she collapsed on to. Loosening her grip on the piece of paper she buried her head in her hands. The tears spilled over and she wept and wept. She had no idea how long she sat on that hard kitchen chair crying for everything that she had lost. Because that is how she felt. She felt as though she had indeed lost everything. If she couldn't see Adam, if she couldn't go to the gigs what did she have left?

When she finally removed her hands from her tear ravaged face the first thing she caught sight of was the picture of Adam and Clare smiling at her from the front cover of that damned magazine. With one movement she snatched it up, pulled off the cover and tore it to shreds.

*

Late pregnancy wasn't easy. Vara had forgotten how uncomfortable it became when you needed a crane to get you off the sofa and you couldn't cut your own toe nails. But although she was struggling physically she couldn't have been happier. The newspaper had just about snapped her hand off when she had offered them the scoop about her pregnancy. She had named her price and was delighted with the amount of money that she had managed to secure. She was now able to buy the flat outright without a mortgage. Not expecting to ever get anymore from Adam she had had to ensure that she was going to have enough to keep her going for quite some time, but being pregnant with Adam Olsen's baby, particularly at the same time as his girlfriend, was of massive interest to the tabloids. The story had only broken today but she had already been approached by several magazines. One of them wanted to do a photo shoot parodying the pictures of Adam and Clare looking into their beautiful crib. The idea was to have Vara standing alone in a shabby room staring wistfully into a grubby looking cot. She had engaged an agent this afternoon to look after her interests and sift through the various offers.

She had been happy with the piece in this morning's paper. It had even made the front page. They had reprinted one of the original pictures of her and Adam together alongside one of her taken now, eight months pregnant. The article had described how Adam had abandoned her, having originally agreed to pay her maintenance, then defaulting after the first payment. They had come to her cramped little flat and taken pictures of her living *in poverty*. They also had a picture of Adam and a very pregnant Clare getting out of the Ferrari.

Everything was back on track now. Daisy and Vara would move into the new apartment within the next week. She fully intended to go down to London for the 02 gig then she would return home and have the baby. Soon after that it would be Christmas. Sighing contentedly she heaved herself up from her seat and headed off to bed. Life in the complex world of Vara Reid was once again good.

*

Day had turned into night. Adam had watched as lights had come on in the properties which were visible across the garden. His studio was now in total darkness. He had seen the children in the house immediately opposite come home from school. He watched as their mother had helped them with their homework and given them their tea. Much later he saw the husband arrive home as his wife was preparing the evening meal. He had seen the obvious affection as he put his arms around her and gently kissed the top of her head. Not a wild passionate embrace, just a tender, loving display of domestic happiness. Normally, if Adam had spent that amount of time observing a snapshot of human life he would have had a song written by the end of it. Sometimes the most successful work came out of the simplest of situations. But not today. Today he couldn't see forward enough to imagine that he would ever write another song again.

He had seen this coming; that was the worst thing about it. Unlike the first time which had taken him totally by surprise. He had known that he was sitting on a time bomb since his return from Russia. But he had been unable to summon up the necessary courage to try and defuse it. So he had just sat back and let it explode. And explode it had. Not for the first time he mused over what he saw as the depravity of tabloid journalists. People who made their living from ruining other people's lives. In his opinion they were barely one step up from criminals. Today they had totally annihilated his character. They had twisted the truth to such a degree that even he barely recognized fact from fiction.

They had made it all sound so credible. Maintenance! They used the word maintenance! What about blackmail? That was the more accurate term. That conniving, scheming little bitch had managed to paint herself as the poor badly done to victim when all along she was the only winner in all of this. He and Clare were most certainly the victims. Swinging around in his chair he grimaced as his thoughts returned to Clare. The feeling of physical sickness that he had been fighting all day threatened to rear up again. Mind you, it would be fairly impossible to be sick when he hadn't eaten anything. He was aware that Helen was upstairs supporting Clare. At least she wasn't alone. He knew that she wouldn't even want to look at him at this stage and he could certainly understand that.

But he did feel victimised. Ok, so up until now life had been pretty kind to him but he was now beginning to understand the old phrase *the higher you climb the harder you fall*.

And he had certainly been brought back down to earth with one almighty bump.

*

Sarah was having trouble focusing. She lay looking at

the geometric pattern dancing in front of her eyes, trying to work out what it was. Slowly she came to realise that it was just the tissue box on her bedside table. Good grief, she must be more screwed up than she thought if she was that confused when she was in her own bed! She sat up and rubbed her eyes, glancing over at a sleeping Dan. She was glad that he was still asleep, it would give her a few minutes to try and collect her thoughts before he woke up and she would have to attempt to sound normal. She felt far from it, the last few days had been very difficult. Dan was, as ever, very accommodating and tried to be understanding but she appreciated that it was difficult for him sometimes to realise how important some things were to her. The 02 gig was tomorrow night, she had an awful lot of money invested in the party on Saturday night and this week the Adam Olsen Fan club had just about gone into meltdown.

All the weekly trashy magazines jumped on the bandwagon and had had a field day literally tearing Adam to shreds. The fans were all over the place in terms of how they had reacted. Being closer to the truth than a lot of them, Sarah was without a doubt, firmly in Adam's camp. She had no doubt whatsoever that Vara had for some reason decided that the time was right to do the dirty well and truly on Adam. Whatever arrangement she had had in place with him had obviously fallen through. She had to hand it to Vara that she timed it to perfection. Adam had a high profile gig coming up and both Vara and Clare were in late pregnancy which created a very emotive reaction both visually and emotionally. Popular culture and media hype being what they were meant that currently Adam Olsen was the most hated man in Britain.

Sarah was worried for Adam. She wondered if he had anyone whom he could turn to for support. She knew that his relationship with Clare had been incredibly close, perhaps closer than a lot of couples. They seemed to do just about everything together. To have that bond torn away from him in the cruelest of fashions must have been devastating. She really couldn't imagine how he was going to come out on stage tomorrow night and put on a brilliant show. She didn't know how the audience would react. Presumably Adam too would be worried about that.

Sarah was also concerned about Janey. She seemed to have fallen off the face of the earth in the last couple of weeks. She wasn't on the forum and hadn't responded to any of Sarah's attempts to make contact. It wasn't like her at all. Sarah wished that she had lived closer so that she could have checked in on her. Oh well, it was the gig tomorrow, she was sure to be there for that. If she wasn't there, well then, Sarah would definitely know that something was seriously amiss and she would go around to Janey's house on Saturday morning. That's all she could do.

Dan was waking and Sarah tried to put her worries to the back of her mind, mentally flicking the switch in her brain from *over-devoted fan* back to *wife and mother*. Sometimes it worked and sometimes it was more difficult than others. Tomorrow as she boarded her flight to London she would be able to switch back fully.

But normally when she travelled to gigs it was with an air of excitement and anticipation. This time it would be with dread and trepidation. What had started a few years ago as fun and an antidote to the trials and tribulations of the real world had somehow become entwined with them.

Trying to hide the worry that engulfed her she wearily climbed out of bed. She didn't know what tomorrow night would bring. All she knew was that she would be there, on the front row, as loyal and devoted as ever. She just wished that she could be sure that the rest of the 23,000 ticket holders would feel the same way.

*

Clare sat in the darkened kitchen. The house had electric shutters on all of the windows for security purposes but they were also perfect for privacy. When they were down the house effectively became a private haven. Or prison. That is what it felt like at the moment. Jason and Helen were the only people whom Clare had allowed into the house over the last week.

Adam had effectively taken up residence in the studio. She heard him moving about sometimes at night, taking a shower or presumably grabbing a few hours sleep in one of the spare rooms on the top floor. But he was never in the house during the day. Jason had been amazing. He had advised Clare on the best course of action regarding privacy and he had arranged for someone to drive Helen around so that she could be there for Clare as much as she could. Not that Clare needed to worry about privacy when she was out as she hadn't stepped out of the door for over a week. It was the worst possible time for Clare to be undergoing stress at this level. Jason was doing his utmost to try and reduce the impact as much as he could. But of course it was almost impossible. Clare was unable to take any form of medication to help her to try to keep calm or even to get some sleep. Physically she was extremely uncomfortable anyway and she felt like she hadn't had a good night's sleep for months. She would have given anything to be able to slip into the oblivion that sleep could bring, into that unconscious state where one didn't have to think about reality.

She looked at the black space where normally she would have been looking out over the top of the Ferrari towards the trees and the open space beyond. Although it was a densely populated area there was a school opposite the house which meant that they looked out over the playing field. Clare had watched the outlook alter this year as the seasons changed and had been excitedly awaiting the winter months as she knew that that meant their baby would be born. Now she just saw the austereness of the metal shutters. She could see no future and it hurt too much to think of the past. The question that had gone through her head so many times since last week was why hadn't he told her? If that woman was pregnant it wasn't going to go away and it was obvious that Clare was going to find out eventually. Ok, so she would never have taken it well, but he could at least have had the courage to tell her to her face. She could never forgive him for not having done that.

He had been paying maintenance. Again, Clare shuddered just as she had done every single time she had thought about that fact. How could he be so involved with somebody to have reached that stage and not told her? She thought that she knew everything about him, just as he did about her. She had never kept any secrets from him. Good grief, she hadn't even needed to tell him that she was pregnant for God's sake, he had already worked it out for himself. He knew *everything* about her. The one thing that hurt her above all else was the thought of another child being in the world that was Adam's.

She accepted months ago that he had slept with that woman and had agreed to move on and not let it bother her. But she couldn't cope with the knowledge that there was going to be another little person in the world who could reasonably call him Daddy. Their baby was so precious to her, and she had assumed that he felt the same. She had had no incline of the fact that elsewhere in the UK there was another woman in exactly the same position as her, pregnant with his child and that he had known about it all along. Clare wondered now how long he had actually known. Had he shown the same intuitive skills as he had with her pregnancy? Had he known for as long as he had known that Clare was expecting? It was just all too much to bear. She couldn't cope with it. She looked at the glass of milk and the plate of fruit that Helen had carefully chopped and placed in front of her. She knew that Helen was desperately worried about her. She was aware that not eating wasn't a great thing in her condition and it was also beginning to affect her ability to think rationally.

But what could she do? There was no magic solution to this problem, no fairy godmother that could grant her three wishes and put the world to rights again. She may be feeling that she was the most badly-done-to person on earth right now and according to Helen, most of the country agreed with her. But it didn't help. Slowly she pulled herself up from her chair and went back to her bedroom. She wouldn't be able to sleep but at least she could rest. That was about all she could do for her poor little baby now. Closing her eyes she began to weep again. Helen, standing at the bedroom door watched helplessly. She quietly walked over and sat down on the edge of the bed. Slowly, rhythmically she stroked her sister's hair and began to hum a soft lullaby just as she did when she was trying to sooth her baby daughter to sleep. Gradually the sobbing became less intense and Clare's breathing slowed down. Satisfied that she was at last asleep Helen gently pulled the cover over her heartbroken sister and quietly crept out of the room.

*

Adam stood on the vast stage staring out at the empty arena. He closed his eyes and took a deep breath. Stay calm he told himself. He really wasn't sure if he was going to be able to pull this gig off tomorrow. He knew that he was not a popular person at the moment. It was, in his opinion, incredibly unfair, but that was the way it was. He accepted that to a certain extent he hadn't helped the situation by burying his head in the sand and hoping that the whole nasty business would go away when it had been obvious that that was never going to happen. But he was outraged as to the way that it had all been blown totally out of proportion. That was why he had decided to end his silence and give his side of the story. This morning before the rehearsal he had gone with Jason and Steve to one of the papers. He had laid down exactly what had happened regarding Vara Reid, how she had blackmailed him and how he had only kept his silence in an attempt to protect Clare. He could see now how foolish that had been but at all times he was just trying to do the right thing.

He knew from his experience after the radio interview following the original newspaper exposé that he would probably receive a mixed reaction. It might win him back a few fans, which would be helpful on the morning of his big gig, but others would think that he was just touting for sympathy. But in all honesty, there was only one person that he was interested in winning over and there was very little chance of that happening. He hadn't seen Clare since last week; he deliberately kept out of her way preferring to wait until she was ready to talk to him. In his heart he was harbouring the slim hope the article would have a similar effect to that of the radio interview. Then, she had forgiven him and leapt on the first plane down to Nice. He knew that the pain was much deeper now and it was going to take more than a few column inches to even begin to start the process of healing. But he was hoping that it might be the first step.

Logistically, everything was ready for tomorrow. The rehearsal had gone well and Jason seemed as happy as was possible in the circumstances. Like Adam, he was extremely concerned as to how things would go. It was impossible to gauge how the audience would react. He had no doubt at all that they would come. Since the story had broken, tickets to the gig had been changing hands for ridiculous amounts on eBay. Human nature could be so cruel. Clearly many people were desperate to see Adam in his hour of suffering. But Adam had never performed in front of a hostile crowd and Jason was worried. Extra security staff had been taken on and everything possible was in place to try and protect Adam. But once he stepped out on to that stage there would be little that Jason could do. Adam would be on his own.

Embracing Adam warmly Jason bid him goodnight. Adam knew the older man was worried 'See you tomorrow Jason,' he called as he headed out to the car. 'It will be fine, you'll see'. Jason watched Adam and Steve climb into the car and pull away. He wished that he could believe Adam's words, he really wanted to. But somehow he just had a bad feeling about tomorrow. Shuddering slightly he hurried back into the building. It was December after all. No wonder he was cold.

*

Adam awoke with a start. He looked at his watch. 10:00am. He sank back onto his pillows as he realised how much his head was hurting. But at least he had slept. It had no doubt been down to the whisky but once he had cleared this headache he would feel much better for having had a night's sleep in a comfortable bed. Last night he had decided that he really needed to try at least to get some proper rest and so had come upstairs to the top floor of the house with his bottle of whisky.

It might not have been a very sensible idea but at least it had worked. He crawled out of bed and went to shower. He stood under the stream of steaming, warm water for a long time, trying to organise the thoughts running through his thumping head. Gig day. Yes, he must get it together. But more importantly, the article should be in the paper today. He was desperate for Clare to see it. He so wanted to have the opportunity to talk to her and hoped that this might be the way in. He would go and buy a paper. The walk would do him good, it would help to clear his head.

As he reached the bottom of the stairs he realised that Clare was in the kitchen. The shutters were still all permanently down. But he realised that they probably needed to be, particularly today. You never knew who would be around on gig days. He stood in the doorway of the kitchen and looked at her. It was only just over a week since he had been face to face with her but it seemed like a lifetime. She looked dreadful, painfully thin but with a huge protruding belly. Her normally sleek glowing hair was unwashed and lank, her skin was sallow and she looked distant, almost confused. He hoped that she was eating but he doubted it. He had managed to have a conversation with Helen the other night. She had said that Clare was unable to eat. He had expressed his concern, not only for Clare but for the baby. Helen had explained that unborn babies were parasites and that they would take their nutrition at the expense of their mother. It certainly looked as though this was the case. He wanted to scoop her into his arms and tell her that everything would be alright. He wanted to take her pain away.

'I'm just going to buy a paper' he said. 'Maybe when I get back we can have a little chat?' His words evoked not even the slightest of reactions, she seemed to be almost in a trance. Giving her a weak smile Adam left the kitchen and let himself out through the front door.

As he walked down the street he remembered that he wasn't supposed to do this. Jason had given him strict instructions not to leave the house on his own. Oh well, he was just walking to the newspaper stand outside the underground station and back. He really did need to clear his head and this was undoubtedly the best way to do it. He would only be out 20-minutes, what harm could come to him in that time? Jason would never know. Wrapping his scarf more tightly around his neck to try to protect his throat and voice from the icy December wind he walked on.

*

Vara parked the car and walked into the service station. She was desperate to use the toilet. With hindsight driving down to London on her own in very late pregnancy really hadn't been one of her better ideas. However, she wasn't prepared to miss the gig and she couldn't face the idea of using public transport in this state. She had reasoned that if she drove she would have the comfort and familiarity of having her own car with her and none of the inconvenience of having to wait around on cold draughty train stations. She had wanted to limit the time that she was away from home so she had got someone in to watch Daisy and had a very early start this morning. At this rate she should get to the venue by about 10.

Having used the bathroom she made her way to the shop. She was doing ok for time so she would check out the latest batch of magazines to see if there were any new articles about her. Then she would get a coffee and sit down for a bit of a break before continuing her journey south. As she made her way towards the magazine shelves she passed the newspapers. There was a picture of Adam on the front page of one of them. This took her by surprise; she wasn't expecting to see him in the papers. As far as they were concerned, he was more or less last week's news. The interest had moved over to the magazines now. It was their job to eke every last drop of juice out of the story. She picked the paper up and quickly scanned the text. The bastard! He had counter attacked with an article claiming that *he* was the victim! She bought the paper, got her coffee and sat down. This was terrible. He was obviously going for the sympathy vote, again. He was good at that. Oh his gig day too. His timing was perfect. How to get the crowd on your side! Vara was furious. Adam had managed to paint her as an evil conniving blackmailer. The bloody cheek of it! All she had ever wanted was enough money to bring her baby up comfortably – a baby that he had helped to create. This was outrageous but it was typical, he was the one with the power. He was rich and famous. Ultimately she was a nobody. That was just the way it worked in this world. The big guys always won in the end. She left her coffee and with tears in her eyes she walked back to her beloved little red Beetle. She unlocked the door and jammed herself in behind the steering wheel. Well, she wasn't turning back now. She would still go to London. She wasn't going to let him off that lightly. She knew where he lived and she was going there.

*

Janey sat in her car in Marlborough Hill. She hadn't been here since she had been served the injunction preventing her from going anywhere near Adam. Not because she was consciously complying with the order but just because she couldn't be sure that he would be here. Particularly after everything had blown up in the papers again regarding Vara, she wouldn't have been surprised if Clare had thrown him out and he was living in some hotel somewhere. Probably in Kings Cross and the whole cycle could start again. Janey sneered to herself. Her feelings towards Adam had changed considerably in the last two weeks. He was no longer the kind considerate golden boy who cared for his fans. He was an evil, selfish, self-important git.

*

Adam was pleased with the article. They had more or

less quoted him word for word. It hadn't been twisted or changed to give a warped impression of what he had said. It was a true account. He re read it several times as he walked back home. His plan for clearing his head had been successful and the good night's sleep had obviously had a positive effect too. He was feeling brighter than he had for days. He would leave the paper for Clare to read then come back after a while and see if he could get her to talk to him. He still had his head in the paper as he turned the corner back onto Marlborough Hill. He liked what he read, it had lifted his spirits and he wanted to keep reading it. Still with his head down he stepped out from behind a parked car onto the normally quiet street.

Adam never stood a chance. All he saw was a flash of red as he was hurtled skyward. The newspaper flew out of his hands and blew in every direction. His crumpled body crashed down onto the tarmac with a sickening thud. Neighbours rushed out of their homes to find his lifeless body lying in the road in a rapidly increasing pool of blood. But there were already people on the scene and one of them made a desperate 999 call whilst the other cradled Adam's ashen face in her hands. Both women were hysterical.

*

Around the corner an elderly gent approached the red car with caution. He was nervous about approaching strangers these days but this heavily pregnant young woman was distraught. She was slumped over the steering wheel and her whole body was wracked with her sobs. He cautiously opened the door and asked if he could help.

Startled and wide eyed Clare stared up at him.

No, no one could help her now.

*

Epilogue

Joshua ran around the garden and clambered up the steps to the top of his small slide. Standing triumphantly on the top rung of the ladder he beamed broadly. 'Look at me Daddy!'

Adam smiled indulgently at his little blond son. He seemed to get braver and more adventurous every day.

'Hey, look at you indeed' he said, moving over to stand nearer to Joshua just in case he became over confident and wobbled off.

'Hurry up Josh,' Chloe was hot on Joshua's heels and wanted her turn on the slide.

The children both shot down the chute and then ran off to play in the sand pit. Adam sat back down on his garden chair, happy that with their feet on the ground they would be safe for a few minutes. No doubt it wouldn't be long before they were off again but for now he had a brief respite.

Clare and Helen came down the steps from the house carrying the lunch that they had just prepared. Clare kissed the top of Adam's head lightly as she reached round him to place the food on the table. He smiled fondly at her. They had come a long way in the last 2 years. His own rehabilitation had been long and difficult but he was getting there. He was just glad to be alive.

Clare had undergone psychiatric treatment and, like Adam, she had had a very difficult path to travel. But with the right care she had begun to accept that her actions on the day of the accident had been a result of her mental health being unbalanced. She was learning to overcome her feelings of guilt. Adam's continued recuperation and growing strength helped with Clare's recovery too.

Vara too had a very different life. Witnessing Adam's accident had been the most horrendous thing that had ever happened to her. She was just eternally grateful that she and Janey had been on the scene so quickly to be able to get Adam the help that he needed. The whole thing had put life into perspective for her. She was *so* relieved that Adam survived. She was happy to live a quiet life with Daisy and her new little daughter.

Janey too had been deeply affected by what had happened in Marlborough Hill that day. Like Vara all she had wanted was for Adam to survive. Thank God he had.

Bonded by their traumatic experience the two women had patched their friendship and nowadays could be found back on the OAFS happily chatting away with Sarah and their other old friends.

Maybe one day Adam would be able to perform again. That was their greatest wish.

And they spent hours and hours and hours talking about it.